"I'm not who ...
he growled

If she hadn't been so terrified, Emily might have laughed. "Next you're going to tell me you're innocent."

"Honey, I'm a long way from innocent, but I don't belong in this hellhole any more than you do."

His voice was like a low rumble of thunder announcing the approach of a violent storm. Emily was aware of his body pressed firmly against hers. She could feel the high-wire tension in his muscles.

"Not another word," he whispered. "Or I swear I'll kill whoever walks through that door."

His gaze fastened on hers and she saw a flicker of an emotion she couldn't quite identify.

"Unless you want me to pull this trigger, I suggest you follow my cue."

Before she could answer, he slid his hands to either side of her face and lowered his mouth to hers.

SAFE HAVEN

LINDA CASTILLO

Operation: Midnight Tango

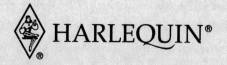

TORONTO • NEW YORK • LONDON
AMSTERDAM • PARIS • SYDNEY • HAMBURG
STOCKHOLM • ATHENS • TOKYO • MILAN • MADRID
PRAGUE • WARSAW • BUDAPEST • AUCKLAND

For George

ISBN-13: 978-0-373-36171-7
ISBN-10:   0-373-36171-8

OPERATION: MIDNIGHT TANGO

LINDA CASTILLO

Linda Castillo knew at a very young age that she wanted to be a writer—and penned her first novel at the age of thirteen. She is a winner of numerous writing awards, including the Holt Medallion, the Golden Heart, the Daphne du Maurier, and she received a nomination for the prestigious RITA® Award.

Linda loves writing edgy romantic suspense novels that push the envelope and take her readers on a roller coaster ride of breathtaking romance and thrilling suspense. She resides in Texas with her husband, four lovable dogs and an Appaloosa named George. For a complete list of her books, check out her Web site at www.lindacastillo.com. Contact her at books@lindacastillo.com. Or write her at P.O. Box 577, Bushland, Texas 79012.

Prologue

The scream echoed off the concrete walls, giving the prison the aura of a medieval castle where unspeakable acts of torture were routine. The prisoner lay on the narrow gurney, struggling against the nylon straps securing his arms and legs, drops of blood staining the sheet covering him from the hips down.

Pain and terror contorted his features. "No more," he whimpered. "Please…"

The doctor in the white lab coat looked down at his charge and reminded himself that the man was a murderer who didn't deserve compassion. But the knowledge didn't make what he was about to do any easier.

Steeling himself against the prisoner's agonized shrieks, he reached for the tiny vial marked RZ-902. "It's almost over," he said. "Just try to relax."

His hand froze on the vial when the door swung open. Tension knotted his stomach when the man in the custom-made suit walked into the examination room.

"For God's sake, I could hear him all the way to

the infirmary." The man scowled at the prisoner. "Shut him up or you're going to have people asking questions we don't want to answer."

"I was just about to sedate him before putting him into the testing chamber."

"Do whatever it takes. Just shut him up. I don't want questions from some do-good corrections officer." Spotting the clipboard on the counter, the man in the suit picked it up and began to read. "How did the patient respond to the RZ-902 treatment?"

Both men knew the words *patient* and *treatment* were euphemisms for something far more sinister. Pushing that thought away, the doctor concentrated on answering the question. "Better than expected."

"The mortality rate?"

"Ninety-eight percent."

"Time frame?"

"Less than five minutes."

"Excellent," the man said, smiling with satisfaction. "I want a full report on my desk within the hour." He glanced at his watch. "I'm meeting with our client at noon. I want all phases of product development detailed."

"I'll get right on it." The doctor nodded as he lifted the syringe to sedate the prisoner.

"No. Please." The prisoner struggled against the straps. "Don't hurt me any more."

The doctor and the man in the suit exchanged looks. The doctor couldn't meet his patient's eyes as he administered the powerful sedative. "Just a little something for the pain," he said as he slid the needle into the man's arm.

"Can't…murder…" The prisoner's voice trailed as the drug seeped into his system.

The man stared coldly at the sedated prisoner. "You made sure he has no ties?"

The doctor nodded. "Just like the others. No family. No friends. He's a lifer and hasn't had a visitor in two years."

"The Bitterroot Super Max has been fertile ground for patients. Make sure it stays that way."

"Yes, sir."

"I'm having another prisoner delivered to you. He should be here within the hour."

"Another patient? Tonight? But it wasn't—"

"I want him given the treatment. Full dose. Make sure the outcome is fatal," he said icily. "Nobody will care if he passes away unexpectedly."

The doctor felt as if a noose were slowly tightening around his neck. "Yes, sir."

"Once you're finished here I want you to take the data you need for the report and destroy everything else. I don't want anything left behind."

Understanding all too well what the man meant, the doctor nodded. "I'll notify the crematorium right away."

"I'm sure I don't need to remind you of the sensitive nature of this project."

"I don't need to be reminded." A man didn't forget about something that tormented him day and night.

When the man left, the doctor wheeled the prisoner into the testing chamber and tried hard not to brood about what he'd done. He tried even harder not to consider what he had to do next.

Chapter One

Zack Devlin jolted awake to the clanging of steel against steel. He was on his feet in an instant, his every sense honed on the two corrections officers standing outside his cell.

"Stand down, convict."

Stand down was the term officers used when they were about to enter a cell. It was a safety procedure that called for a convict to lace his fingers, then put his hands behind his head. What were two corrections officers doing in his cell in the wee hours of morning?

Zack assumed the position, his heart racing. "Isn't it a little early for tea and scones?" he asked.

The first corrections officer was Mitchell. He treated the convicts with a firm hand but never unfairly. The other officer was about as pleasant as a bad case of the flu. He liked to tear down a man's dignity. Maybe even hurt a man if he got the chance.

Mills's keys jangled as he unlocked the cell door. "Step back."

Zack did as he was told, but his nerves were on edge. Both men entered his cell. "If I had known you were coming, I would have tidied the place up."

"Shut your smart mouth and show me your wrists," Mills said sharply.

The Bitterroot Super Max Prison was a place of routine. Day after day after day that routine never altered. Two corrections officers coming into his cell at four in the morning and cuffing him was definitely not part of the routine.

"What's this all about?" he asked, trying to sound casual.

"Turn around," Mills repeated. "Now."

Knowing he didn't have a choice, Zack turned and offered his wrists for Mills to snap the nylon restraints into place. The thought that his cover might have been compromised floated through his mind. But he knew that was impossible. The agency had been meticulous in setting up the assignment and his background. There was no way anyone could know.

"Spread your legs."

Zack wasn't wearing a shirt. Just a pair of wrinkled drawstring pants that were issued to all the inmates for sleeping. "Not much room to hide a weapon," he said.

"Just following procedure. Do it."

Never taking his eyes from Mills, Zack did as he was told. He ground his teeth as Mills's hands moved swiftly and roughly over him.

"He's clean." Mills grasped the restraints and shoved them up and between Zack's shoulder blades. "You're going to the infirmary."

Zack's heart rolled into a fast staccato. He was all too aware what went on in the prison's infirmary. What the hell was going on? "I'm not sick."

"Doc says you need a blood test."

"I don't need a blood test."

Mitchell tapped the clipboard he held. "Got the order right here, partner. Let's go."

"What's the blood test for?" Zack asked, his mind spinning through all the scenarios that could be waiting for him in the infirmary. None of them were good.

"You can ask the doc when you get there. Now move it."

The instinct to fight was strong, but any attempt to make a stand or run would be futile. He'd learned to choose his battles since arriving at the prison four months ago. Experience told him this wasn't one he would win. He couldn't stop remembering all the other inmates who'd gone into the infirmary and come out bloody or burned—or not at all.

He glanced at the clock on the wall. In another hour he was supposed to rendezvous with his contact from MIDNIGHT. Zack had a sinking feeling he wasn't going to make it. When it came to the prison infirmary, a single hour could mean the difference between life and death.

As they guided him down the corridor, he figured he had about two minutes to come up with a plan. But then, he'd always been able to think fast on his feet.

He only hoped he came up with something fast enough to save his life.

AT FOUR IN THE MORNING, the prison corridors were as dimly lit as an underwater cave. Emily Monroe's boots echoed off of concrete and steel as she hurried toward the infirmary. Her shift didn't begin until five, but she'd come in early to do some poking around in the infirmary. She had plenty of questions that needed answering. Like what had happened to the two inmates who'd gone into the prison infirmary and never returned to their cells. Since Dr. Lionel didn't seem disposed to explaining, she figured she'd just have to get the answers on her own.

At the end of the corridor, she swiped her security card, then punched the four-digit code into the keypad set into the wall. The steel lock snicked, and she shoved the door open.

The prison infirmary was as dark and silent as a tomb. Odd, since the facility was manned twenty-four hours a day, seven days a week. The utter quiet gave her a prickly sensation on the back of her neck.

Puzzled, she tiptoed to the second door that would take her to the inmate receiving area, the procedure rooms and inmate holding cells. She swiped her card, watched the red light change to green and opened the door. She found the interior as still and dark as the rest of the place. At the very least she'd expected Dr. Lionel's graveyard-shift assistant to be in her office, working on her computer. Where was everyone?

Growing increasingly apprehensive, Emily rested her hand on the pepper-spray canister clipped to her belt and started down the hall. The soft thud of her boots kept perfect time with her heart, which was beating far too quickly.

She passed exam room one and flipped on the light. She saw an examination table, stainless-steel counters and a pull-down light. But not a soul in sight.

Emily didn't scare easily, but in the three years she'd worked as a corrections officer in Idaho's Bitterroot Super Max Prison she'd learned to trust her instincts. Right now those instincts were telling her something was terribly wrong.

Shoving open the door to exam room two, she turned on the light and spotted the outline of a man beneath a sheet splattered with blood on the examination table. Crossing to the table, she peeled away the sheet. Apprehension zinged through her when she saw the waxy flesh of the prisoner's face. His blue lips. A thin line of blood had trickled from his nostril and dried black. His eyes were partially open. He was dead.

Queasy with fear, she touched his face. His body was still warm. What was going on here? Where was Dr. Lionel and his assistant? What had happened to this inmate?

She thought again of the other inmates who'd gone into the prison infirmary and vanished. For weeks she'd been asking questions and making inquiries, but no one in a position of authority had given her a straight answer. This morning she'd taken matters into her own hands and come here to have a look around. She hadn't expected to find a dead body....

Struggling to remain calm, Emily tugged her

radio from its sheath. "This is zero-two-four-niner. I've got a code—"

Movement from behind her cut her words short. She spun. The blue steel of a gun flashed. She saw black hair. Dark eyes. An unshaven jaw. A hot jet of adrenaline burned through her. Gripping the radio, she brought it to her mouth. "Code—"

A hand snaked out and ripped the radio from her grasp. In her peripheral vision she saw it sail through the air. She lunged toward the door, but in an instant the man was upon her, his hands encircling her biceps before the radio even hit the floor.

"Don't make a sound if you want to live," he said, his eyes glittering with threat.

Emily broke his hold and jumped back. "Stand down, convict! Do it now!" She tried to sound authoritative, but her voice held a damning quiver of fear.

"Stay calm and don't fight me." He started toward her. "I don't want to hurt you."

She didn't know if it was the gun in his hand or the look in his eyes, but for a single, terrible instant she was frozen with fear. An inmate armed and desperate with absolutely nothing left to lose was every corrections officer's worst nightmare.

She stepped back, raised her arms to stop him, knowing they wouldn't. "Get away from me."

He didn't stop. "Just do as I say and you won't get hurt."

She barely heard the words over the rapid-fire beat of her heart. She looked at the gun in his hand, measured the distance between them, the distance to the door. She wondered if she could reach her radio on the floor before he shot her in the back.

An instant later her training kicked in. Springing forward, she kicked the gun from his hand. The weapon clattered to the floor. Before he could pick it up, she tried a palm-heel strike to his face, but he blocked it. Spinning, she lashed out with her left foot, landing a kick to his abdomen. Grunting, he reeled backward. She then reached for the canister of pepper spray clipped to her belt. She brought it up while simultaneously diving for her radio. She had to get to that radio!

He moved with the speed of a big, hungry cat taking down its prey. In a single smooth motion he scooped up the gun and spun toward her. With his free hand he slapped the canister of pepper spray from her grasp. The next thing she knew, his hands were on her shoulders, digging into her flesh, and she was being shoved backward into the examination room.

"For a corrections officer, you don't take orders worth a damn," he growled.

"Get your hands off me!"

"Calm down and listen."

A yelp escaped her when her back hit the wall. She was pinned. She tried to use her knee, but he shifted sideways, blocking her attempt to disable him. She squirmed, but his body was as hard and unyielding as a brick wall against hers. "Unless you want to end up like that man on the table, don't try that again," he warned.

His voice was low and dangerous. She detected an accent. Irish maybe. But she was too scared to think too hard about it. His face was only inches from hers. So close she could feel the warmth of his breath against her cheek. She stared into eyes the color of dark-roast coffee, saw deadly intent and desperation and realized he wasn't the kind of man who made idle threats.

"You can't possibly think you're going to get away with this," she said breathlessly.

"That's exactly what I think." Every nerve in her body jangled when he shifted away and leveled the gun on her chest. "Get your hands up."

Emily raised her hands to shoulder level. "I'm not armed."

"Nothing personal, but I'd rather make that determination myself." Never taking his eyes from hers, he ran his hands quickly and impersonally over her body, pausing when he discovered the extra canister of pepper spray strapped to her ankle. Damn.

"Guess you forgot about this."

"I like to be prepared in case I get jumped by some piece-of-scum convict."

She spotted blood on the underside of his wrist as he tossed the canister into the trash container. Not an abrasion he might have sustained in a scuffle but a clean slice. The kind of incision a doctor would make for a surgical procedure. She wondered if he'd overpowered Dr. Lionel during some kind of minor surgery.

"Where's Dr. Lionel?" she asked.

"We don't have time for questions." He motioned toward the door with the gun. "You're coming with me. Let's go."

"Where are you taking me?"

He was wearing only a pair of prison-issue drawstring pants. No shirt. No shoes. He was built like a distance runner, with long limbs and an abdomen that looked as if it had been carved from stone. His chest was rippled with muscle and covered with a sprinkling of black hair. He was grace and power rolled into a single disturbing package.

Tearing her gaze away, she tossed a covert glance at her fallen radio a few feet away. If she could reach it, all she needed to do was hit her personal alarm button and alert dispatch that she was in trouble....

"Don't even think about going for that radio," he said. "I don't want to hurt you, but if you force my hand, I will."

She met his gaze levelly. "You don't want to do this."

"What I don't want is to become one of Dr. Jekyll's guinea pigs."

Dr. Jekyll's guinea pigs? Emily didn't know what he meant by that. The guy was obviously delusional. She knew better than to engage him, but if she could talk him down, she stood a better chance of coming out of this unscathed. "You don't stand a chance of getting out of here. Even if you make it out of the building, the tower guards will be all over you."

"I'll take my chances with the guards. They're a

hell of a lot less lethal." He gestured with the gun toward the door. "Let's go."

She led him from the exam room to the interior door, but her hands were shaking so violently she could barely swipe her security card. Once the green light flickered, she tugged open the steel door and took him into the darkened hall. She sensed the presence of the gun as she walked, the almost tangible aura of danger surrounding the man as she took him into the main corridor.

"I need a uniform and coat," he said.

She started to protest, but he raised the gun and aimed it at her face. "Get them for me," he said. "Now."

In his gaze she saw violence and unpredictability and understood that if she didn't do exactly as he said he would kill her. "The locker room," she said.

"Take me there—and make it fast."

They took the corridor at a run with Emily in the lead. She hoped desperately for a fellow corrections officer to appear, but the shift hadn't yet ended and this particular corridor was deserted.

By the time they reached the locker room, she was breathing hard and sweating—partly from the exertion, partly from fear. The locker room was a narrow tiled room that smelled of dirty socks. One wall was lined with a double row of slate-gray lockers, the other with stainless-steel shelves, matching hooks for towels and coats and gear. A wide doorway opened to the shower room.

"Find me a uniform."

Emily crossed to one of the lockers. The convict stood behind her while she removed a uniform and shoved it at him. "Take it and go."

He took the neatly folded shirt and pants, then stepped back and set the gun on the bench. Never taking his eyes from hers, he hooked his thumbs around the waistband of his own pants. "Don't even think about running," he said. "I shoot just as well naked as I do clothed."

Ridiculously embarrassed, she averted her gaze as he stepped out of his pants. Clothing rustled. For a crazy instant she considered making a run for it. But while Emily was fast, she wasn't fast enough to get through that door without risking a bullet in her back.

She stole a look at him out of the corner of her eye. He'd picked up the gun and was buttoning the shirt with his left hand, holding the gun on her with his right. The shirt was a tad too large but passable. In the darkness of early morning, he would pass as a corrections officer.

"Put on your coat," he said.

She jolted at the sound of his voice. He was dressed now, right down to the cap and boots. Only he had a gun. A gun he'd vowed to use if she didn't do exactly as she was told.

"I'm not going anywhere," she said.

"Put it on," he snapped.

Emily didn't want to go with him. She sure as hell didn't want to help him escape. It went against everything she believed in, everything she'd been trained for. Worse, it triggered memories of what her father had done, and she'd sworn she would never disgrace herself the way Adam Monroe had.

She watched as he began searching through the coats hanging on the racks. Her eyes flicked past him to the alarm panel set into the wall near the door. Panic-button panels were located throughout the prison and available for officers to use in the case of an emergency or crisis—such as the one she was facing now. If she could reach it…

Emily stared at him, her heart hammering against her ribs. She was standing midway between him and the alarm. If she moved quickly, she could slam her fist down on the button before he could stop her. Within minutes a dozen corrections officers would descend, and this man would have no choice but to surrender.

Crossing him was dicey. There was the very real possibility that he would kill her. After all, the federal government didn't put nice guys in the Bitterroot Super Max. This prison was reserved for the most violent, dangerous prisoners.

Her vision tunneled on the protruding red button. Her pulse skittering wildly, she sidled closer, one inch at a time. With four feet to go, she launched herself at the alarm.

An instant before her fist made contact with the button, viselike arms wrapped around her waist. "Code *three!*" she screamed and rammed her elbow into his gut.

A hand over her mouth cut off her words, then he

pulled her away from the alarm and swung her around. Emily used every ounce of strength and every self-defense tactic she'd learned over the last three years. But he was incredibly strong and over-powered her with an ease that amazed her.

The next thing she knew, her back connected with the lockers. The breath left her lungs in a rush of air that was part growl, part scream. "Get your hands off me!"

"If you want to live, you'll shut your mouth and listen!" Holding her against the lockers, he glanced over his shoulder toward the door, as if expecting someone to rush them at any moment. When he turned back to her, his eyes were dark with anger. "What are you trying to do? Get someone killed?"

"I'm trying to keep a dangerous convict from es-caping," she said.

"I'm not who you think I am," he growled.

If she hadn't been so terrified, Emily might have laughed. "Next you're going to be telling me you're innocent."

"Honey, I'm a long way from innocent, but I don't belong in this hellhole any more than you do."

His voice was like the low rumble of thunder an-nouncing the approach of a violent storm. Emily was aware of his body pressed firmly against hers. She could feel the tension in his muscles, the quiver of nerves raw with adrenaline.

The thud of shoes against concrete sounded out-side the door. His body went rigid. "Not another word," he whispered. "Or I swear I'll kill whomever walks through that door."

She could feel the butt of the gun against her belly. "Don't," she said. "I'll do whatever you say."

His gaze fastened on hers, and she saw a flicker of an emotion she couldn't quite identify. Just as quickly as it had appeared, it was gone, leaving her to wonder how this was going to end. If he was going to kill her. If he was going to kill one of her co-workers. If she would have that death on her conscience the rest of her life.

He stared at her for an interminable moment, his expression a disturbing mix of fear and very dark intentions. "Unless you want me to pull this trigger, I suggest you follow my cue."

Before she could answer, he slid his hands to either side of her face and lowered his mouth to hers.

Chapter Two

Emily was so shocked by the sudden intimate contact that for a moment she could do nothing but stand there and try to absorb what was happening. She was keenly aware of his mouth against hers, of the forbidden rush of pleasure that surged from her lips all the way to her toes.

Somewhere in the back of her mind an internal alarm wailed. Some small voice of reason telling her to shove him away. But the heat of the kiss was interfering with the synapses firing in her brain. Every impulse to scramble back and forget this had ever happened was tempered with a stronger impulse to kiss him back and worry about the consequences later.

His mouth was firm and breathtakingly talented against hers. She could feel the warmth of his breath on her face. The scratch of his stubble against her cheek. When she opened her mouth to voice the protest caught in her throat, he deepened the kiss.

Her protest came out as a sigh. She could feel her

body melting. She knew it was the worst thing she'd ever done in her life. But the sensations coursing through her overwhelmed her, made her think maybe kissing him was a mistake worth making....

"Monroe?"

With a strength that surprised her, she shoved the inmate away, appalled by what she'd done, stunned by what she felt, mortified by how this would appear to a fellow corrections officer.

That officer was standing at the locker room doorway, his gaze sliding from her to the inmate and then back to her. "Is there a problem here?"

"No," the convict said.

The young officer addressed Emily. "Where's your radio?"

Heat infused her cheeks. She didn't know what to say. Didn't know what to feel. Barely able to meet the other man's gaze, she stepped away from the inmate. "I—I must have put it in my locker."

The officer glared at the inmate with narrowed eyes. "Who the hell are you?"

The convict grinned like an idiot and stuck out his hand. "Zack Devlin," he said.

Reluctantly the officer took his hand. "You new or what?"

"First day on the job." Devlin whistled. "Hell of a facility you've got here."

"Yeah, well, if you want to keep your job, I suggest you keep your mouth to yourself." The man disentangled his hand and glared at Emily. "The sergeant has been trying to reach you on the radio.

We've got a situation in Cell Block 2-W. Code yellow for now, but I expect them to crank it up to red if the second head count comes up short. Sarge has asked every officer on duty to stay until they find the missing inmate."

"Oh…uh…sure. I'll just…get my radio and meet up with you in the briefing room."

"And bring the new recruit with you." Sending a final scathing look at Zack, the officer turned and left the room.

Emily's knees went weak the instant the other man disappeared, and she sat down hard on the bench. She couldn't believe what she'd done. Couldn't believe one of her co-workers had seen her do it. What had she been *thinking* letting an inmate kiss her?

Groaning, she put her face in her hands. "I'm finished as a corrections officer."

"Look, if I hadn't done what I did, you would have brought down the wrath of God knows how many corrections officers, and I'd be on the floor getting a mouthful of concrete about now."

Raising her head, all she could think of was that she was twenty-eight years old and she'd never been kissed like that in her life. Suddenly she felt as much contempt for herself as she did for the inmate.

He glanced toward the door. "Look, things are about to get nasty. I'm going to go while the going is good. I appreciate the help."

"Don't thank me for something I didn't do," she said, giving him a seething look. "I'm going to hit the alarm the moment you walk out that door."

"Just remember that things aren't always what they appear," he said. "No matter what you hear about me later, don't forget that."

No, Emily thought, she didn't think she would ever forget this night no matter how much she wanted to.

"Watch your back." Giving her a mock salute, he slid through the doorway with the soundless grace of a panther and disappeared into the dimly lit corridor.

For several seconds Emily sat motionless on the bench and listened to the hard pounding of her heart. She couldn't believe what had just happened. Couldn't believe levelheaded Emily Monroe had fallen for the oldest con in the book. She'd dishonored herself, jeopardized her job and compromised everything she'd ever believed in.

Just like her father.

She rose on trembling legs and started for the alarm panel. She was midway there when movement at the doorway drew her attention. For an instant she thought Devlin—or whatever his name was—had returned. She was surprised to see, of all people, Marcus Underwood, the administrator of Lockdown, Inc., the private corporation that ran the Bitterroot Super Max. What on earth was he doing at the prison this early in the morning?

"Mr. Underwood," she said. "I was just—"

"Officer Monroe." He crossed to her, followed by another man. "We caught part of what happened on the security cameras from the command center. Are you all right?"

"I'm fine," she said.

"You're aware that we're currently under a code yellow."

"Yes, sir. I was about to hit the alarm. An inmate overpowered me in the infirmary less than ten minutes ago." Her voice shook as she described the situation she'd walked into at the infirmary. "He identified himself as Zack Devlin."

The two men exchanged a look that sent a chill up her spine. "Devlin has a long and violent history," Underwood said.

"Did he get away?" she asked.

"Nobody gets away from Lockdown, Inc." The second man came up beside Underwood. The stripes on his shoulders told her he was a lieutenant, but she'd never met him. "We'll get him."

Underwood addressed Emily. "Did he tell you anything? Mention where he was going?"

She shook her head. "All I know is that he's wearing a Lockdown, Inc. uniform and coat and that he's armed with a semiautomatic pistol."

"How did he get a weapon?" Underwood asked no one in particular.

"Evidently he had help," the lieutenant said. "Someone must have smuggled it in."

"Zack Devlin could talk a nun into lying for him." Underwood looked grim. "Put out a code red."

"Yes, sir." The lieutenant reached for his radio and began barking orders.

Hearing the squeak of rubber against concrete, Emily turned to see a man in a white lab coat standing in the doorway.

"Ah, Dr. Lionel," began Underwood. "Before we take Officer Monroe to the debriefing room for a statement, we thought it would be a good idea for you to look her over, make sure she's all right." He turned his attention to Emily. "You've been through quite an ordeal with a very dangerous criminal. Lockdown, Inc.'s policy requires you to be thoroughly checked out by one of our medical personnel."

"I'm fine." She just wanted to get the paperwork finished so she could go home and forget this ever happened.

The three men were staring intently at her. Emily started to tremble when she noticed the syringe in Dr. Lionel's hand. "What's that for?" she asked.

Underwood gave her a reassuring smile. "I can see that you're upset. You're still shaking. Dr. Lionel is just going to give you a little something to help you relax."

"I don't need to relax." Emily didn't know what was going on, but there was something very wrong with this picture. As crazy as it sounded, she couldn't shake the suspicion that these men hadn't appeared out of nowhere to help her or debrief her. But why would they harm her? What could they possibly have to gain?

"What's this all about?" she said. "What's going on?"

Underwood spoke. "Did Zack Devlin tell you anything, Emily?"

Warily she glanced from man to man. "I've already told you everything that happened."

"Everything, Emily? Are you absolutely certain? We were watching you on the security cameras, you know. You and Devlin seemed to be quite…close for having just met."

The kiss, she thought and closed her eyes briefly. *Dear Lord, they think I helped Devlin escape.* "I—I can explain what happened."

"Please do."

"H-he surprised me. I was so…stunned, I couldn't react."

"Do you have any idea what the penalty is for aiding and abetting an escaped convict?" the lieutenant asked.

"I…didn't," she said breathlessly. "I wouldn't do that."

"Your father did."

Humiliation cut her at the mention of her father, but she kept her shoulders square, her chin up. "I know how this might look, but I did not help that man escape."

"Someone did," the lieutenant said.

"I followed policy and procedure," she maintained.

"Of course you did." Underwood assumed the classic good-cop role. "And now you're going to tell us what Devlin told you."

"He didn't tell me anything."

Sighing as if she'd disappointed him, Underwood nodded at the doctor.

"What are you doing?" she asked as the doctor approached her.

His grim expression raised gooseflesh on her arms. "We're going to give you a little something to help you remember."

Emily couldn't believe this was happening. She stared at the syringe in Dr. Lionel's hand, her heart pounding like a drum. The three men stood squarely between her and the door. There was no way she could get by them. Her hand went to the canister of pepper spray that should have been clipped to her belt only to find it gone. Damn. Damn. *Damn.*

"I want to speak to Warden Carpenter." She'd known Clay Carpenter since she was a teenager. He'd worked with her father a decade earlier. The two men had been friends. He'd helped Emily get her job at the prison. He would never approve of what these men were about to do.

"I'm afraid the warden is unavailable," the lieutenant said.

"Stay away from me," she warned.

In tandem the lieutenant and the doctor closed in on her. "Don't make this any more difficult than it already is," the doctor said.

Emily lunged toward the alarm panel. Two sets of hands closed around her biceps and yanked her back.

"Let go of me!" She lashed out with her feet.

"This will be easier for you if you cooperate," Underwood said. "Tell us what Devlin told you."

She looked over to see Dr. Lionel thumb the cap off the syringe. "Keep that away from me!" she yelled, hoping she didn't sound as terrified as she felt.

"We're not going to hurt you, Emily. This is just a little thiopental sodium to help you tell the truth."

Truth serum, she thought with a burgeoning sense of horror. "You can't do this."

Grabbing her arm, the lieutenant shot an irritated look at the doctor. "Inject her, damn it. We don't have much time."

The doctor raised the syringe. Emily had worked for Lockdown, Inc. for three years. She had two commendations in her personnel file. Why didn't they believe her? Why would they go to such great lengths to extract information when she didn't have a clue what they wanted from her? What could possibly be important enough to risk Lockdown, Inc.'s reputation? Or even her life?

Just remember that things aren't always what they appear.

Devlin's words scrolled through her mind. She glanced at Dr. Lionel. The needle was about to penetrate her skin. Oh, dear God…

"The first man that moves gets a bullet for his trouble."

The doctor froze. All eyes swept to the doorway. Zack Devlin entered, his gun leveled on Underwood. He looked at Emily. "You okay?"

"No." She scrambled back, looked from Zack to Underwood, then back to Zack. "I want to know what's going on."

"You were about to become Lockdown, Inc.'s latest victim." His gaze cut to Underwood. "Killing your own people now?"

"You'll never get out of here alive," the lieutenant sneered. "Nobody has ever escaped this prison and lived to tell about it."

"I've always had a knack for breaking protocol." Devlin's mouth curved in a dangerous imitation of a smile. "Get facedown on the floor. Hands behind your backs. All of you. *Now.*"

"He's a killer," Underwood said to Emily as he got down on the floor. "Don't believe anything he says. You're through, Devlin!"

Ignoring him, Zack crossed to her and held out his hand. "Give me your cuffs."

Numb with shock and the knowledge that she was about to cross the point of no return, she removed three nylon restraints from her belt and handed them to Zack. She watched as he secured the men's hands behind their backs.

"What are you doing?" she asked.

"Saving your life." He shot her a sober look. "And mine. Come on."

Underwood raised his head. "Don't ruin your life, Emily. You don't know who you're dealing with. Zack Devlin is an Irish terrorist. A very dangerous man who's murdered dozens of innocent people."

Zack reached for her hand, but she stepped back, out of his reach. "I'm not going anywhere until I know what the hell is going on," she said.

"They think I told you something." He gazed levelly at her, his expression unreadable. "They were going to pump you full of truth serum."

"Why did you come back?"

"Because after they injected you, they were going to kill you."

Shuddering, Emily looked at the three men lying facedown on the floor. She'd known Marcus Underwood for three years. She couldn't understand why a man of his stature would resort to such tactics. What could she possibly know that could be of value to him?

On the other hand, she'd seen the syringe. There was no doubt Dr. Lionel had been about to inject her with truth serum. Did they suspect Zack had given her some sort of sensitive information? Did they think she had smuggled that gun in and helped him escape? How was she supposed to make sense of any of this?

"You have to trust me." Zack said the words with cold calm, but she heard the skitter of nerves just beneath the surface. "They'll kill you if you stay."

"Give me one good reason I should go with you," she said.

He shot a pointed look at the clock on the wall. "For starters, in about thirty seconds all hell is going to break loose."

Emily was absolutely certain all hell had *already* broken loose. She was wondering how the situation could get any worse when an explosion rocked the building.

Chapter Three

"Run!"

Zack didn't wait for her to obey his command. Grabbing Emily's hand, he dragged her from the locker room and into the main corridor.

A deafening alarm screeched intermittently, keeping perfect time with the blinking red strobes that ran along the walls. He tightened his grip on her hand and tugged her toward the personnel tunnel that would take them to the parking lot where a four-wheel-drive SUV waited, compliments of his contact at MIDNIGHT—a man Zack would happily kiss right now if he were around.

Unfortunately Emily was more interested in answers than running. Digging in her heels, she yanked her hand from his and turned on him, her expression frightened and angry. "What did you do?" she demanded. "What did you blow up? If you hurt someone—"

"I didn't hurt anyone," he cut in.

"I heard the explosion, damn it."

"You heard a variation of a concussion grenade. All I did was add the timer. A lot of noise and smoke but no fire. It's a diversionary tactic."

"Why should I believe anything you say?"

"Maybe you prefer to go back in there with those nice men who were about to inject you." Turning to her, he put his hands on her shoulders. When she tried to pull away, he squeezed just hard enough to make her hold still, listen to him. "Look, we don't have time to discuss this. All you need to know is that you're in danger. If we don't get out of here pronto, they're going to kill us."

"Why?"

Because of me, he thought bitterly, and a hefty dose of self-recrimination rose inside him. The memory of Alisa's death pressed into him with sharp, cruel fingers.

Shoving thoughts of the past back, he looked over his shoulder. "In a few seconds this place is going to be teeming with men who've been given orders to kill us on sight. If we don't get through the personnel tunnel now, we're toast."

She looked pale and shaken despite the tough veneer she wore like a coat of armor. He could feel her shaking beneath his hands. Zack couldn't blame her for being afraid, for not believing him. She thought he was a convict trying to escape. But he could tell she had good instincts. That those instincts were telling her to believe him. If he could only get her to listen to them.

"Trust me," he said urgently. "I'll tell you as much as I can once we're safe."

She didn't pull away when he reached for her hand. They sprinted down the corridor at a reckless speed, rounded a corner and entered another hall. Ahead, two corrections officers manned the metal detector all personnel had to walk through to reach the tunnel.

Stopping abruptly, Zack lurched back, out of sight. "Damn it."

"What's wrong?"

"Metal detector." He tugged the gun from his waistband, looked at it longingly, then tossed it into a darkened corner. "Let's hope this goes the way I want it to."

Both men looked up as Zack and Emily approached. A quiver of fear went through him when they raised their shotguns.

"Hold it right there," the first man ordered. "Show me your badges. Now."

Zack reached into his coat for the ID he'd stolen back at the infirmary. The photo on the badge didn't look anything like him, but all he could do now was hope the officer didn't notice.

"Hell of a night for a code," he said casually.

"Ain't that the truth," officer number two muttered.

Vaguely Zack was aware of Emily holding out her badge, the officer looking closely at it, his shotgun ready at his side. Zack unclipped his own badge and held it out. He tensed as the officer looked at it, then at him. "That's not your photo," he said.

"Sure it is," Zack returned smoothly.

The second officer came around the metal detector. "There a problem?"

Zack laughed. "Says this photo doesn't look like me. Guess I'm too good-looking for my own good."

The man eyed him suspiciously. "Where you headed?"

For the first time Emily spoke up. "Sarge sent us to do a perimeter patrol of the parking lot. Keep an eye on the vehicles." She glanced at her watch. "We gotta run, boys, so make up you minds if that looks like him or not."

Frowning, the officer passed the badge back to Zack. "Go."

Zack didn't have to be told twice.

THE PERSONNEL TUNNEL TOOK them to the employee exit. Emily hit the push bar on the double door and shoved it open. The cold predawn air hit her like a blast from a freezer, and she shivered.

"Where to now?" she asked.

"Keep walking."

But midway to the parking lot Devlin stopped, as if listening, and looked over his shoulder toward the prison. "This is too easy. They had to have seen us on the cameras."

"If they'd seen us, we'd be in custody already," she said. "The SORT team doesn't mess around." The SORT team was the prison system's version of a SWAT team.

"Unless their intent isn't to take us into custody."

For a moment the only sound came from their

boots sinking into snow as they jogged across the parking lot. Around them the January night was bitterly cold. The occasional snowflake fell from a black sky, but the air was heavy with moisture, a precursor to a heavy snowfall.

"Over there." He pointed toward a big white SUV parked in the far corner of the lot.

"Now you're adding grand theft auto to your repertoire of charges?"

"My contact left it for me. There's a GPS chip and a few other useful items hidden inside the wheel." Taking her hand, he started toward the vehicle at a dead run. "Hurry."

Contact? GPS system? Useful items? A dozen alarms were blaring simultaneously inside Emily's head, most of which were warning her not to believe a word he said. She didn't know what was going on or who to trust. The one thing she *did* know for certain was that this man was a convict. That he was escaping. That her employers at Lockdown, Inc. presumed she was helping him.

But she couldn't explain what had taken place back in that locker room. Would Marcus Underwood and his men have hurt her if Zack hadn't shown up when he did? What information could he possibly have that would be so valuable? Emily didn't know the answers, but the possibilities chilled her to the bone.

When they reached the SUV, Zack went directly to the right front tire and knelt to open a small hidden compartment set into the wheel. Emily stared in shock as he withdrew a good-size drawstring satchel and a set of keys. She'd never seen a key holder like that before. "How did you know that was there?"

Grinning, he tossed the keys into the air and caught them with one hand. "Must be my lucky day."

The tinny *thwack!* of a bullet penetrating steel punctuated the statement. *Thwack! Thwack!*

"Get down!"

The next thing Emily knew, she was being shoved to the ground. She got a mouthful of snow, and then Zack was on top of her. *Thwack! Thwack!* His body jerked with each gunshot. She could feel her own nerves jumping, terror beginning to flood her. *Thwack!*

"Damn it!"

She looked up to see the right front tire explode. Then her hand was locked within his and she was being dragged to her feet. "Run!"

She heard fear in his voice. Felt that same fear galloping through her own system. Adrenaline fed her muscles and within a few steps she was running full-out.

"Where to?" Zack shouted.

"My car. In the lot."

"We're sitting ducks in the lot."

The pop of gunshots sounded behind them. Floodlights as bright as the sun flashed on. The outdoor sirens began to wail. Emily looked over her shoulder and saw a dozen men silhouetted against the prison walls.

"They're shooting at us!" she said.

"I don't know why that would come as a surprise."

Something that felt like a red-hot baseball bat traveling at the speed of sound slammed into her upper arm. She yelped at the sudden burst of pain. The impact knocked her off balance. Her legs tangled. Zack's hand was torn from hers as she went down hard on her stomach.

"Emily!"

She lifted her head, saw him rushing toward her, his face taut with horror. She had snow in her eyes. In her mouth. In her hair. Down the front of her shirt. For some reason, her arm was burning like the dickens.

"Are you hit?" He went to his knees beside her, reached for her, pulled her toward him. "Are you hurt?"

"No. I mean, I don't think—"

"Damn it!"

She looked over to see his fingers probing the tear in her coat. Now how had *that* happened? Weren't the SORT team marksmen supposed to be shooting at Zack? Since when had she become a target? "Oh, my God."

"You've been shot." He glanced over his shoulder, cursed. Four men in full SORT team assault gear were two hundred yards away and closing fast. "Can you run?"

"I don't think I have a choice."

Pulling her to her feet, he looked around. "We need a vehicle."

"The utility garage." She pointed with her good arm. "Over there."

"Let's move." Taking hold of her uninjured arm, he tugged her into a run toward the corrugated-steel utility garage.

One of the four overhead doors stood partly open. Emily and Zack ducked under the door and burst into the building. Country music billowed from a radio atop a toolbox. Two ATVs were parked near the first bay. A small yellow bulldozer hulked in the corner. Two four-wheel-drive trucks with the Lockdown, Inc. logo on the doors sat at bays two and three.

A scrawny young man wearing insulated coveralls looked up from the engine he was working on. His face blanched at the sight of Zack. "You're the escapee," he said.

"I'm your worst nightmare if you don't find us a vehicle pronto," Zack said.

The young man looked as if he were about to swallow his tongue. "Take whatever you want." He pointed. "If it were me, I'd go for the snowmobile. Weatherman says we're going to get dumped on."

Wondering what else could go wrong, Zack darted to the snowmobile, shot a hard look at the kid. "Where are the keys?"

The young man raised a trembling hand and pointed. "O-on the bulletin board," he squeaked.

Emily crossed to the bulletin board, snatched the keys off a hook and tossed them at Zack. He caught them with one hand, then said, "If you know what's good for you, you'll run out that door and forget you ever saw us."

The wrench the kid was holding clattered to the floor. Backing away, he spun and sprinted through the door without looking back.

Emily watched him disappear into the falling snow. She could hear voices and shouting coming through the open door. No doubt the prison SORT team and tower guards were assessing the situation. It was only a matter of minutes before they stormed the place.

Somewhere in the distance an engine fired. She watched Zack pull a small bundle from the satchel and set it on the floor beneath one of the trucks.

"Give me that gas can," he ordered.

Emily spotted the red can next to the workbench, picked it up and handed it to Zack. "What are you doing?"

"Just taking out a little insurance." He placed the can next to the bundle, then dashed to the snowmobile, picked up two helmets and slid onto the seat. "Come here."

She met him at the snowmobile. Her arm was burning and throbbing. Light-headed, she wondered if the wound was more than just a graze.

"You okay?" Eyeing her intently, he lifted one of the helmets and slid it gently onto her head.

"Oh, I'm just peachy. In the last half hour I've been taken hostage, shot at, lied to by people I thought were the good guys. No, I'm not okay! I want to know what the hell is going on."

His eyes met hers as he fastened the strap beneath her chin. "Look, I didn't mean to involve you. But

I can't leave you here. And there's no time for me to explain right now, okay?"

It wasn't okay, but she didn't think it would help the situation if she started demanding answers now. She looked down at the hole that had been torn in her coat. Her stomach clenched when she saw the blood seeping through the sleeve.

As if reading her thoughts, Zack reached out and touched her arm. "As soon as we get out of here, I'll find a place to stop and take care of your arm. I'm an EMT. I won't let anything happen to you."

It was ridiculous, but looking into his eyes, she believed him. "I can't believe they shot me." Of all the things that had happened, that was the one that bothered her the most. She'd been a member of the Lockdown, Inc. corrections team for three years. Her teammates were her friends. Her *family.* Surely the prison marksman had been aiming for Zack.

Hadn't he?

His eyes darkened as he slid his own helmet over his head and fastened the strap. "I'm going to drive this thing like a bat out of hell. Put your arms around my waist and don't let go. You got that?"

The motor purred like a big, wild cat as she slid onto the seat behind him and wrapped her arms around his waist.

An instant later the snowmobile's steel shoes dug into the concrete. Sparks flew as the machine shot out the open door like a cannonball.

Once outside, Zack looked behind him toward the utility garage, holding what looked like a tiny television channel-changer in his hand. He depressed a button, then dropped the device into his coat pocket. "Hang on!"

The snowmobile took off like a racehorse out of the gate. Emily tightened her arms around Zack's waist. She heard gunshots and shouting over the roar of wind coming through her helmet. Zack veered sharply, barely missing a light pole. They were heading toward a line of trees that would take them to the foothills of Idaho's Bitterroot Mountain range when the garage exploded.

Even from a hundred yards away Emily felt the hot breath of the explosion. She glanced over her shoulder to see a ball of flames billow like a giant orange mushroom into the early-morning sky.

"I take it that wasn't a concussion grenade," she shouted to be heard over the whine of the engine, the roar of wind around her helmet.

"No," he shouted over his shoulder. "But it might buy us some time if we're lucky."

"If we're lucky?"

"Yeah." He muttered a curse. "We're about to run out of gas."

"How could this happen?" Marcus Underwood furiously paced the briefing room.

Standing a few feet away, Lieutenant Riley Cooper looked everywhere but into his superior's livid eyes. "We didn't anticipate an inmate getting inside help," he said.

"Didn't *anticipate?* It is your job to anticipate!"

The other man swallowed hard. "I understand."

"I want them caught or dead—and I want it done yesterday!"

"Y-yes, sir."

The seven men who comprised the prison SORT team shifted uncomfortably in their chairs while their team leader was grilled to a crisp.

"The woman, too?" one of the men asked after a moment.

"She is an accomplice and is to be considered armed and extremely dangerous. For God's sake, she smuggled a firearm into the prison for him." Underwood's gaze scanned the faces of the team he'd gathered to hunt down and kill Zack Devlin and Emily Monroe. "All of you saw the security-camera video. She and Devlin have evidently been planning his escape for quite some time. He is armed with explosives, antipersonnel devices and at least one semiautomatic weapon. I don't need to remind any of you what this man is capable of."

Nobody had anything to say about that. Underwood had made certain each man on this handpicked team had seen the file he'd built on the infamous Irish terrorist, Zack Devlin. As far as they knew, Devlin had spent the last ten years murdering indiscriminately. Men. Women. Children.

"This is a race against time, gentlemen," Underwood said. "It is your responsibility to stop this murderer and his accomplice before they kill again. It is your responsibility to bring them back to me dead or alive. Am I clear?"

Silence shrilled for the span of a full minute.

"This briefing is over," Underwood snapped.

The team members rose quickly, gathered their weapons and gear and filed out the door.

Dr. Lionel was in the process of gathering his notes when Underwood approached him. "Were you able to locate and remove the GPS device before he got away?" Underwood asked.

"It had been implanted just under the skin." The doctor pulled a sealed plastic bag from the file and held it up. "I extracted it just a few minutes before he overpowered me."

Underwood took the bag and studied the tiny device. "Looks to be state of the art."

"It is. But without it, whatever agency he's working for won't be able to locate him."

The lieutenant approached the two men. "Devlin doesn't stand a chance in a storm like this with seven of my best men tracking him."

"You had better be right." Underwood looked at Dr. Lionel. "I do not want our progress on RZ-902 interrupted."

The doctor nodded. "We're moving on to the next phase as planned."

"Excellent. You know how I feel about delays." Dropping the GPS device on the floor, Marcus Underwood crushed it with his shoe. "I hate waiting almost as much as I hate loose ends."

Chapter Four

Zack pushed the snowmobile to a dangerous speed, zipping between trees and treacherous outcroppings of rock. The machine beneath him screeched like a mechanical banshee. Wind and snow battered his body and face shield. Even over the roar of wind he could hear the rotors of the helicopter overhead. He could see the spotlight sweeping down like a white tornado. If they were spotted, it would be over. Not only for him but for the woman he'd dragged into this.

Cursing beneath his breath, he punched off the single headlight. Behind him Emily tensed. "You can't drive this thing without headlights!"

There was no other choice. The headlights made them sitting ducks. Blanketed in darkness, it took all his concentration to steer around the trees and jutting rock. He silently prayed he wouldn't run them into some immovable object. At this speed, an accident would be fatal.

"I know what I'm doing," he said.

He remembered from the map he'd studied of the area surrounding the prison that the main road leading to the small, rural town of Salmon was straight ahead. He was familiar enough with law-enforcement tactics to recognize they were setting up a perimeter. That there would be roadblocks. The map had shown a less-traveled dirt road that would take them west into the Bitterroot Mountains. The terrain would be rough, but with a chopper hovering just a few hundred yards away, Zack didn't have a choice but to take it.

The road forked. Without slowing down or hesitating, Zack veered left. Trees and rock formations blew past as he pushed the snowmobile at a reckless speed down the narrow road. He was putting them in a perilous position, but getting shot at seemed even more dangerous, so he leaned forward and put the pedal to the metal.

There were no towns to the west. Just the vast wilderness of the Salmon National Forest. If they were lucky, they might be able to find a ranch and get to a phone. But even if they did, Zack wasn't sure whom to call. Clearly someone at the agency had sold him out. He didn't have a clue who or why. But he was going to find out. And then he was going to take great pleasure in breaking every bone in their body.

Of course, before he could do that he had to stay alive. That meant losing the chopper.

He ducked instinctively when the powerful spotlight swept over them. He twisted the throttle, trying to squeeze more power from the snowmobile, but the engine was running at its peak. Damn it!

The spotlight swept over them again, only this time it held.

"They've spotted us!" Emily cried.

"Not for long," Zack fired back. "Hold tight."

He swerved right and for an instant they were hidden beneath the canopy of pines that grew along the road. But the spotlight latched onto them again when they burst from the cover of the trees.

Snow being kicked up from the chopper's rotors blinded him, but Zack held the handlebars steady and managed to keep the snowmobile on the road using the treetops as his point of reference. The chopper was flying low and bearing down on them, getting closer and closer....

Suddenly a bullet blew a hole through the Plexiglas windshield. Fear notched up into cold, hard terror at the realization there was at least one sharpshooter on board the chopper. And that he and Emily were in his crosshairs. He didn't know if there were enough trees up ahead to provide ample cover. If he didn't do something quickly, they would be shot....

Then the windshield exploded. Plexiglas blew back, pelting his face shield and chest. Through the driving wind and snow Zack spotted an opening in the trees off to his right. "Hang on!" he shouted and drove off the road.

The snowmobile bumped over some fallen logs and snow-covered rocks the size of basketballs. He felt Emily tighten her grip. Even through the pandemonium of the out-of-control ride and the knowledge that certain death was only a tiny miscalculation away, Zack vowed to keep her safe. She might be employed by Lockdown, Inc., but he didn't think she was involved with the RZ-902. She sure as hell hadn't asked for this.

A rock the size of a Volkswagen came at them seemingly out of nowhere. Zack turned hard to the left. The snowmobile tilted at a precarious angle, but he leaned into the turn and managed to keep it upright. He glanced behind him, looking for the chopper, and saw with some surprise that it was nowhere in sight.

"Do you see the chopper?" he shouted.

"I think it went straight when we went into the trees," Emily answered.

That wouldn't last long. Chances were, the Lockdown people were equipped with night-vision equipment. They probably had infrared technology, as well, which worked much the same way only using body heat instead of light. In the snow, he and Emily would stand out like neon beacons.

Zack glanced down at the gas gauge, which had been on E since leaving the prison maintenance building. The best he could hope for would be that they had enough to get them out of the immediate area.

The trees had opened up and Zack drove the snowmobile like a madman. Even though the headlights were off, he could see that they'd entered what looked like an old ski slope. The terrain was sloped severely, but it was clear of trees for the most part. He took the snowmobile up the mountain at an angle.

The snow was coming down in earnest now. If the bad weather continued, there was a good possibility the chopper would be grounded. If they could reach a house or flag down a passing motorist, they might just get out of this alive.

The hope evaporated like a snowflake in the sun when the snowmobile jerked violently. Too late Zack saw the looming cliff. He applied the brake and yanked the handlebars hard to the right. Snow spewed high into the air as the big machine pivoted. To his left he saw the black vastness of space, but they were still on solid ground. For a moment he thought they were going to make it. Then the snow crumbled beneath them.

"Jump!" he shouted to Emily.

The warning came too late. The snowmobile plummeted downward. The engine whined as the machine went into a free fall.

Emily screamed. The terror in her voice pierced him like a dagger. He wanted to turn to her, tell her he hadn't meant for this to happen. He hadn't meant for her to get hurt….

Then the snowmobile tumbled into a nosedive, and Zack couldn't do anything but pray.

EMILY WASN'T SURE how or when she'd lost her grip on Devlin; she'd been holding on tightly just a moment before. Now she was flying through the air, barreling toward an inevitable impact that would surely kill them both. Damn convict. If she'd had a gun, she would have pulled it out and shot him.

She slammed into the ground hard and lost her breath. She heard a crash nearby, then the world went silent and still. For several seconds she lay there, trying to get oxygen into her lungs. When she opened her eyes, she saw heavy snow swirling down. The tops of the pines were swaying. She could hear the wind whistling through the branches.

She'd fallen into deep snow, which had cushioned her fall. Shifting slightly, she took a quick physical inventory and ascertained she was relatively injury-free. Groaning, she rolled onto her side, sat up and looked around.

She was sitting on a steeply sloped incline in two feet of snow next to a broken sapling pine and a big chunk of the snowmobile's fairing that had been ripped off in the fall. Twenty feet away the snowmobile lay on its side, the engine sizzling and smoking like an overcooked steak.

Slowly Emily got to her feet. Her arms and legs shook as she brushed the snow from her clothes. She glanced up and saw they'd gone off the cliff and down about twenty feet. A long way to fall. She was fortunate to have survived unscathed and wondered if Devlin had been so lucky.

"Devlin?" she called out.

She stood motionless and listened for a response, but none came. Even though Devlin was an escaped convict who had taken her hostage and nearly gotten her killed, the thought of being out here in the middle of nowhere all alone was unnerving. Especially since she was becoming more and more certain there was something sinister and deadly going on at Lockdown, Inc.

She was going to have to climb down to where the snowmobile lay to check on Devlin. Emily started toward the ledge. "Devlin, you had better be alive," she muttered beneath her breath as she plowed through deep snow. "Because I'm going to wring your neck with my bare—"

The sound of a breaking twig cut her words short. Gasping, Emily spun—and found herself staring into Zack Devlin's eyes. For the first time since he'd taken her hostage, he looked shaken. His face was pale against his dark hair. Blood was trickling down from a cut at his temple. How badly had he been injured?

"Are you hurt?" he asked.

The question took her aback. She didn't expect him to be worried about her well-being one way or another. "Considering you just tried to kill me by driving off a cliff, I'd say I'm doing better than expected. What the hell were you trying to pull?"

"Maybe you'd rather take a bullet in the back."

She didn't have a comeback for that. Whomever had been in that chopper *had* been shooting at them. And they hadn't seemed too concerned about which of them they hit. A deeply disturbing fact.

"If it hadn't been for me, your pals back at the prison would have turned you into Swiss cheese," he said.

"They were shooting at you," she said. "In case you're wondering, that's standard operating procedure when an inmate takes an officer hostage and escapes."

He glanced away from her and looked up at the sky as if gauging the storm. He had a strong profile with a straight nose and chiseled mouth. Emily wasn't sure why, but the sight of his lips made her think of the kiss in the prison locker room. Remembering it right now was ridiculously inappropriate considering the situation. But neither of those things changed what the kiss had done to her….

Tearing her gaze away from him, Emily brushed the last of the snow from her coat and slacks and looked around. Under different circumstances she might have enjoyed the beauty of the night. The heavy snowfall was lovely against the backdrop of the mountain forest and night sky. But standing out in the middle of nowhere with an escaped convict who'd nearly gotten her killed removed any discernible pleasure.

"We lucked out," he said. "The chopper must have been grounded because of the storm."

"Oh, yes, I'm feeling luckier by the second," she said dryly. "If we're really lucky, we'll be buried alive with snow by morning."

The look he gave her caused the hairs on her arms to prickle. A different kind of uneasiness rose inside her. Emily wasn't familiar with his background or what he'd done. It had to be brutal, savage, for him to end up in the Bitterroot Super Max.

She didn't want to think about what he was capable of. Or what he might do to her...

Refusing to let the thought spook her, she stuck out her chin and gave him a hard look. "So what do you propose we do now, Einstein?"

"First and foremost, we stay alive."

That might be very difficult under the circumstances. Emily refused to go there.

He sighed, motioned toward the tear in the sleeve of her coat. "At some point I'll need to take a look at that bullet wound."

Between dodging bullets and crashing the snowmobile, she'd pushed the pain in her arm to the back of her mind. But now that he'd mentioned it, she could feel the stinging and burning of the bullet wound, the wet stickiness of the blood.

"Why don't you just make a run for it while you can?" she said.

Her heart sped up when he stepped close to her. "Because I didn't risk my life breaking out of that hellhole to run."

"You don't need me," she said. "Just go and leave me here."

"If they find you here or anywhere else, you're as good as dead."

"They wouldn't—"

"They would," he said sharply. "Do you think that bullet wound in your arm was an accident?"

"I think the SORT team marksman was trying to stop you. I got in the way."

"In case you've forgotten what happened in the

locker room, let me refresh your memory. Three men. One of them had a syringe with your name on it. He was going to shoot you up with some kind of truth serum, for God's sake. Then who knows what was next on the agenda."

Emily wanted to deny it but couldn't. She'd seen the syringe. She'd seen the looks on the men's faces. And she'd known what they'd been about to do. But why?

"They think I helped you escape," she said dully.

"They think you know something you shouldn't."

"Like what?" she asked.

"Like why inmates at the Bitterroot Super Max have been dying under mysterious circumstances for the last six months."

Something was going on at the prison. In the last six months, she'd personally known of at least two inmates dying unexpectedly. That was why she'd been asking questions. That was why she'd been in the infirmary that morning to begin with.

But to believe the people she'd worked with for the last three years were capable of murder was unthinkable. How did Devlin know about it? There appeared to be a lot more to Zack Devlin than met the eye.

"How do you know inmates have been dying?" she asked.

"I know because for the last four months I've watched men systematically disappear. Healthy men who are sent to the infirmary. Most come back to their cells deathly ill. Some of them don't come back at all."

Was Devlin just a smooth-talking liar whose very freedom hinged on manipulating her into helping him?

But in her heart Emily knew *something* was going on at the prison. She just didn't know what.

Things aren't always what they appear....

"What's happening to them?" she asked, her voice dropping to a whisper.

He turned his gaze to hers. She saw a weariness that hadn't been there before and wondered about its source. "Horrors you can only imagine in your worst nightmares," he said.

Emily stared at him, aware that she was frightened. And that the fear didn't have anything to do with the man standing so close she could see the stubble on his cheek. Deep inside she knew that despite whatever this man might have done, he was not lying about Lockdown, Inc.

"Who are you?" she asked.

"I'm the man who's going to try to save your life, if you'll let me."

"You're a dangerous fugitive. You've taken me hostage—"

"And you'd be dead right now if I hadn't gotten you out of there."

"You can't possibly know that."

"They would have killed you the same way they've killed countless others in the last six months."

Looking suddenly tired, he raised his hand and touched the cut on his temple. His lips pulled into a frown when his fingertips came away red. He wiped it on his slacks and looked around. "Look, we need to put some distance between us and that prison. Then we need to find shelter. I have a feeling the weather is going to get worse before it gets any better."

"I deserve an explanation."

"You deserve to stay alive." He turned to her, his expression tense. "They're probably putting together a search team as we speak."

"No professional in his right mind would send out search teams in this storm."

"No, but a madman would. The people at Lockdown, Inc. have too much at stake to let us get away."

"You keep using the term *us,*" Emily choked out. "Unless you have a mouse in your pock—"

"Like it or not, you are now on Lockdown, Inc.'s most-wanted list. Your only chance of coming out of this alive is to stick with me. If the storm doesn't get too much worse, we might be able to outdistance them. Then maybe I can get us some help."

"Help from whom?"

He looked away, his jaw flexing, as if her question had more ramifications than she'd intended. "We've got to go," he said. "In another hour there may not be any visibility at all." He shot her a look that made the hair at her nape prickle. "That's the best-case scenario, Emily. If the weather improves, this area is going to be crawling with heavily armed cops with itchy trigger fingers. If they get their hands on us, we're going to wish we hadn't survived the plunge off that cliff."

Chapter Five

Zack tried to restart the snowmobile, but the tumble down the cliff had damaged both the track shoes and the engine. After wasting precious minutes, he abandoned the idea and he and Emily set off on foot.

It didn't take long for him to realize that neither of them was dressed for hiking in severe weather conditions. No hats. No gloves. No waterproof boots. It would be only a matter of time before the cold took its toll in the form of frostbite or hypothermia. Two problems Zack figured they could do without considering the mountain was swarming with armed men bent on killing them.

"What the hell else can possibly go wrong?" he muttered as he trudged through knee-deep snow.

"Mother Nature could always make things a little more interesting."

Zack shot Emily a sour look, annoyed because she was right. In the last hour the wind had picked up, whistling through the treetops like a thousand teakettles. The snow was coming down sideways.

His ears were cold. His feet were numb. And as much as he didn't want to admit it, he was pretty sure they were lost.

He'd memorized the map given to him by his superior at MIDNIGHT as he'd prepared for the mission. Avery Shaw had made certain Zack had had everything he needed for the operation. Maps of the prison. Terrain maps of the surrounding area. Background reports on Lockdown, Inc.'s employees and inmates.

A bloody lot of good those things were doing him when he couldn't see but a few feet in front of his face.

But Zack knew most storms in this part of Idaho blew in from the northwest. He and Emily were heading into the wind, so he could assume they were heading northwest. He recalled seeing a notation on the map that there was an abandoned ski lodge somewhere in the area. It had been popular back in the 1960s but later abandoned. Hopefully the old place was still standing. If he and Emily were really lucky, there would be no welcoming committee from Lockdown, Inc. waiting to gun them down.

A few feet away he could see Emily struggling through the wind and deep snow. Even though she seemed to be in relatively good physical condition, she was smaller and suffering from a bullet wound. He could only imagine how grueling this was for her.

"I think there's an old ski lodge ahead," he shouted to be heard above the roar of the wind.

Through the driving snow he saw her glance his way. "You mean the old Capello Hills Lodge?"

"Is it still standing?"

"Barely. I've never seen it, but a couple of the other corrections officers hiked up there last summer while on a rock-climbing excursion."

Zack tossed her a furtive glance. She was only a few feet away, but he could barely make out her silhouette in the blinding snow. Dangerous conditions for even the most seasoned outdoorsman. It would take only an instant for them to become separated. Ideally he would tie a rope to her. Since he was fresh out of rope, he opted for the next best thing.

"Give me your hand!" he shouted, walking toward her.

Even with the poor visibility he saw the astonishment on her face. "What?"

"So we don't get separated." Without waiting for her to respond, he reached for her.

She initially resisted, then her hand relaxed within his. Her skin was like ice. Lord in heaven, she was nearly frostbitten.

Wishing he could do something to keep her warm, he tugged her along at a faster pace. "Let's make some time," he said, praying he could find the lodge before it was too late.

DAWN BROKE AS DARK AND gray as a partial solar eclipse, but the light did little to improve visibility. The snow was still coming down hard, and visibility had dwindled to less than five feet. If it hadn't been for the shift in the pitch of the whistling wind, Zack would have walked right past the Capello Hills

Lodge without even seeing it. But from twenty yards away, he discerned the change as the wind whipped around the portico. Finally they'd found the shelter they so desperately needed.

"Jackpot," Zack said.

Emily had been lagging behind for the last hour. Zack hoped her slow pace was due to the punishing conditions and not the bullet wound. He wasn't particularly fond of corrections officers at the moment, but he didn't want her hurt. One woman's death on his conscience was about all he could handle....

Not allowing himself to think of the past, he took her to the open area beneath the portico where the building blocked most of the wind. Capello Hills Lodge had obviously once been magnificent, but no more. The glass in the front windows was long gone, replaced with plywood that had weathered badly. The once-rustic siding was warped and rotted. Some joker had nailed a No Trespassing sign to the front door.

Not bloody likely, Zack thought and tore the sign from its nails and tossed it into the snow. He tried the door but it didn't budge. He couldn't tell if it was locked or warped, but he wasn't going to let either of those things keep him out.

"Stand back," he said.

Emily moved away. "We could try the ba—"

Zack landed a single solid kick to the door. It swung open. Dust motes exploded when it banged against the wall. Wishing for his sidearm, he stepped inside and motioned for Emily to follow.

He closed the door behind them, then stood quietly and listened, hoping they were alone. He could still hear the storm raging outside, but the sudden silence of being out of the wind was profound enough to make his ears ring. He turned to Emily to tell her to stay put while he took a look around, but the sight of her stopped him cold. Her hair was wet and she was shaking furiously. Her face was ghastly pale. She probably wouldn't have lasted much longer out in the cold.

"You're bloody hypothermic," he said, his voice coming more roughly than he'd intended.

"I'm j-just c-cold."

He took her arm to guide her to the massive hearth. She surprised him by shaking off his touch and glaring at him. He found himself staring into eyes the color of aged whiskey. Her mouth was full and sensuously shaped, like a pale ruby set into ivory. The combination of those two things socked him in the gut like a fist, and he found himself wanting to do a hell of a lot more than just touch her….

"In case you haven't noticed," she said, "I'm cold and wet and very ticked off. I've been shot at and lied to by people I once trusted. I've been driven off a cliff. Dragged through a snowstorm by an escaped convict. And I have a bullet wound in my arm." Eyes flashing, she stepped closer to him and jammed her finger in his chest with enough force to push him back a step. "I want to know what the hell is going on. And I want to know right now."

Zack stared at her for an interminable moment.

A measure of relief went through him when he saw that some of the color had returned to her cheeks. He wondered how long that would last once he told her what her pals back at Lockdown, Inc. were up to.

She wasn't going to like it, but she deserved the truth. Thanks to him, Marcus Underwood and his army of goons were trying to kill her, too. Now it was Zack's responsibility to keep her safe.

The thought twisted his gut, made him feel a little sick. The last time he'd tried to keep a woman safe, she'd ended up dead. Would he fail Emily, too?

"I'm going to build a fire," he said. "Then we'll talk."

EMILY WATCHED ZACK FEED wood to the fire blazing in the floor-to-ceiling river-rock hearth and tried not to relive everything that had happened in the last four hours—and not to imagine what might happen next. Born and raised in this part of Idaho, she'd seen enough winter storms in her life to know that no one was going to show up to rescue her. Not the police. Not the FBI. Not even the highly trained prison SORT team employed by Lockdown, Inc.

She was on her own.

What she needed more than anything was answers. She needed to know who Zack Devlin was and why he'd taken her hostage. Even more, she needed to know why the prison marksmen had been shooting at her. Why Marcus Underwood and Dr. Lionel had been within an inch of injecting her with truth serum. Why inmates were mysteriously dying...

Shuddering at the possibilities, she looked across the room at Devlin and wondered what secrets were buried beneath all those layers of Irish charm. Was he a dangerous, cold-blooded killer? Who was he really?

Things aren't always what they appear....

What had he meant by that?

"That ought to keep us from getting hypothermia."

Emily looked up at the sound of his voice to see him standing a few feet away, watching her with an unnerving intensity. The irises of his eyes were so dark they were nearly black. A day's growth of stubble shadowed his jaw. The cut on his forehead stood out in stark contrast against his skin. Having worked the last three years as a corrections officer in a maximum-security prison, Emily had dealt with plenty of ruthless, brutal men. But staring into Zack Devlin's glittering eyes, she thought he seemed by far the most dangerous.

They studied each other for an uncomfortable moment. Emily could hear the wind tearing around the old lodge. Something flapped rhythmically against the exterior window, like a ghost hammering at a nail. The entire place seemed to shudder with every gust of wind.

But even though the man standing across from her radiated danger, she felt strangely safe....

"Why don't you have a seat by the fire and let me take a look at that bullet wound?" he said.

The thought of getting closer to the fire appealed, but Emily was nervous about Devlin touching her—for reasons she didn't want to acknowledge.

"Look," he said. "I don't know how long we're going to be stuck here. If that wound is bad, it could get infected and make you sick."

He was right. An untreated bullet wound could lead to infection, which could be serious. "As long as you can talk and administer first aid at the same time."

"I'll see if I can find some supplies I can use to get it cleaned up." Turning away, he strode through an arched doorway.

She watched his retreat, then rose and wandered around. The main room was cavernous, with high ceilings and massive rustic beams. Arched windows ran from floor to ceiling. The floor was made of parquet and stone and littered with years of dust and small debris. Holes marred the walls where fixtures and wall hangings had once been. But it was the stone hearth that dominated the room. Forty years ago the place would have been magnificent.

The scent of burning wood hung pleasantly in the air. Despite the fire, the room was still freezing, so she crossed to the bench he'd dragged to the fireplace and sat. The warmth felt wonderful against her skin. Her feet were numb. She looked down at her hands. They were red and aching from cold. Her hair and coat were damp. She was in the process of taking off her coat when Zack returned, his hands full.

"This must be our lucky day," he said.

Emily didn't feel very lucky. In fact, she thought this was one of the worst days of her life. "Did you find first-aid supplies?" she asked.

"I melted a little snow in this plastic container. I found a bar of guest soap. And last but not least, a bottle of vintage 1981 cognac."

"I don't think cognac is going to help our situation."

"Quite the contrary."

She tensed when he sat on the bench beside her and began to open the bottle. "This isn't for drinking, though I might just have a nip considering the age of this bottle."

"If you're not going to drink it, what do you plan to do with it? Blow up something?"

"Cognac has a high volume of alcohol," he said. "It will burn like the dickens, but it will disinfect your wound." One side of his mouth hiked and he grinned like a scoundrel. "If you're game, we can drink the rest."

Emily refused to let herself be charmed. This man had taken her hostage. Thrown her in the line of fire. Risked her life to save his own. *Kissed you like you've never been kissed before,* an annoying little voice reminded. The memory of the kiss heated her cheeks. She desperately wanted to deny the effect it had had on her. But Emily had always been honest with herself, and Zack's kiss had moved her in ways no other kiss ever had in all of her twenty-eight years. What kind of woman enjoyed a kiss from a convict?

Like father, like daughter….

For most of her adult life she'd hated her father for what he'd done. For giving into weakness and disgracing the uniform he'd worn. For humiliating himself and his family. Was she like Adam Monroe?

"Looks like you've lost a good bit of blood."

His words dragged her from her painful reverie. Emily looked over to see him fingering the bullet hole in her coat. Sure enough, the material was saturated with drying blood.

"I'm going to roll up your sleeve and take a look now, okay?" he asked.

She nodded, but still she flinched when he touched her.

"Hurt?" His fingers brushed against her arm as he rolled up her sleeve.

"What do you think?" Her stomach roiled at the sight of the bruised flesh and clotted blood.

"It's not too bad," Zack said.

"You're only saying that because it's not your arm."

"I'm saying that because it's a scrape. It bled a lot, which is a good thing. You've got some bruising, but not much tissue damage. It's basically a flesh wound."

"You sound as if you're speaking from experience."

His hands stilled on her arm, his gaze meeting hers. "Maybe I am."

He dipped a small towel into the pan of water and dabbed at the wound. Because she didn't want to look at it, Emily watched his hands. She couldn't help but notice they were incredibly gentle.

Using the towel, water and soap, he scrubbed the wound. She tried not to wince, but the pressure hurt. "Sorry," he said. "I just need to make sure there are no foreign particles inside the wound that might cause infection later on."

She wished he wouldn't apologize for hurting her. Inmates weren't supposed to be nice. They weren't supposed to have a soft touch. Or the kind of hands that made a woman want to lower her guard.

But Emily never lowered her guard. Not in her professional life. Never in her personal life. She had learned at a very young age what could happen when you did.

"This is going to sting."

Zack's words pulled her from her thoughts. She looked up to see him uncap the bottle, then drizzle a small amount of cognac over the wound. The pain was instantaneous and fierce, as if someone had dropped a burning ember directly into the wound. Emily ground her teeth, but she didn't utter a sound.

He stroked her arm with his thumb as he blotted the excess liquid from her skin. His touch was as smooth and gentle as his voice. "You okay?"

She shot him a hard look. "I'd be a lot better if you told me who you are and what's going on."

"My name is Zack Devlin. I'm an agent for a branch of the CIA known as MIDNIGHT. Four months ago I was sent undercover to Bitterroot because over the past year alone at least twelve inmates have died under suspicious circumstances. My assignment was to find out why these inmates died and who's responsible."

Emily was aware that her heart was racing. That her hands were shaking. And that despite the heat of the fire, she was cold again all the way to her bones.

"I've never heard of MIDNIGHT," she said when she found her voice.

"MIDNIGHT is a secret agency within the CIA. We take on the missions no other agency will touch. The missions nobody ever hears about on the six-o'clock news."

"I can't believe an agency would jeopardize one of its agents by sending him into a maximum-security prison like Bitterroot."

Never taking his eyes from hers, Zack removed his jacket, then rolled up his sleeve to reveal a deep precision cut. One that had bled every bit as profusely as hers, yet he'd never said a word. Emily remembered seeing the blood that morning when he'd accosted her in the prison infirmary. She'd assumed he'd overpowered Dr. Lionel during a minor surgical procedure. Now she wasn't so sure.

"My superior at MIDNIGHT takes every precaution to make sure his agents are safe." He glanced down at the wound, which was located on the underside of his left arm. "I had a Global Positioning System device surgically implanted before this mission in case something happened and the agency needed to locate me quickly. Earlier this morning two corrections officers came into my cell, cuffed me and took me to the infirmary, where the device was removed."

"How did they know it was there?" she asked.

His expression darkened. "The only logical explanation is that my cover was compromised."

Because she hadn't yet decided if she believed him about his being an undercover agent, she went to her next question. "Why are the inmates dying?"

"The less you know about—"

"Don't give me that," she cut in. "I need to know everything."

He sighed heavily, then looked away from her to stare into the fire. "The Bitterroot Super Max Prison is the largest privately run prison in the country. As a corrections officer, you're probably aware that the facility is inspected at the state and even federal levels, but that doesn't mean those inspections are thorough. And it doesn't mean things can't be hidden."

"Things like what?"

He turned his gaze to hers, and for the first time Emily saw the spark of a very dark emotion she couldn't quite read.

"You know what kind of men end up at Bitterroot," he said. "Murderers. Rapists. It was designed for the most violent offenders. In many cases, their friends and family have either disowned them because of what they've done or have simply grown tired of Sunday visits and have fallen out of touch.

If something were to happen to those inmates, there would be no one to ask any questions."

"What are you saying?"

"A year ago MIDNIGHT was approached by another agency. Some checking of the prison records revealed that several inmates had died under mysterious circumstances. Inmates with no one to question…or even take notice of their deaths. MIDNIGHT tried to assess the situation by sending in operatives posing as government inspectors. But the people at Lockdown, Inc. guard their secrets well. They're tight with information and even tighter with what they tell their own employees and management. As a last resort, my superior approached me with the idea of my going deep undercover, and I accepted the mission. I was thoroughly briefed. A fake identity was created documenting my so-called crimes in police and court records. Then I was sent into the prison population as an inmate."

Emily's mind was reeling. "What's happening to the inmates?"

"I believe Lockdown, Inc. is using inmates to test chemical weaponry."

She knew most of the corrections officers. She knew Dr. Lionel and Marcus Underwood. She knew Warden Carpenter.

"There's no way something so…heinous would be condoned by Lockdown, Inc."

"I've seen the results, Emily. Healthy men sent to the infirmary for some minor problem return deathly ill. Some of them suffering from horrific skin lesions. Others with severe respiratory illnesses. Healthy young men bloodied and poisoned and screaming in agony when they're brought back to their cells. And those are the lucky ones, because most don't return at all."

Emily could barely absorb what he was saying. Never in a thousand years could she have imagined something so cold-blooded. To think that the people she had known and worked with for three years were capable of such utter brutality made her sick to her stomach.

Rising abruptly, she paced over to the hearth and leaned against the cool stone. "How can you possibly know all of that? You were an inmate. You were not privy to infirmary records."

He hesitated for an instant. "I'm not the only operative working out of Bitterroot."

"But who else—"

"That's classified information."

"That's convenient."

"For your own safety. If Underwood thinks you know something and gets his hands on you, believe me, he'll use any method available to him to find out what I've told you." He looked away, his jaw taut. "Including torture."

A chill rippled through her.

"The inmates see a hell of a lot more than you think," he said. "They talk. We're talking about men who've led violent lives. These men don't frighten easily. But I've heard the talk. And I've heard the screams. I've seen hardened, brutal men cowering like frightened children in the months I was there."

"Why didn't this get reported? I mean, we have an inmate relations officer—"

"An officer who may very well be part of it. You think anyone is going to open his mouth and risk being tortured to death?"

The scenario made her shudder. "Who is Lockdown, Inc. testing weapons for?"

"I don't know," he said, frustration evident in his voice. "But I suspect there is a company somewhere in the United States manufacturing the chemical agent. From there, the agent is shipped to Bitterroot for testing. Once the weapons are deemed effective, they'll hit the black market. Worldwide. Lockdown, Inc. receives money for their part, and no one will be the wiser. Bitterroot is the perfect location. Remote. Isolated. No residents nearby to notice the supplies being trucked in and out daily. It would be easy for such an operation to continue without interference."

"Who ships the weapons?"

"We don't know. But as you can imagine, there are plenty of terrorist organizations and rogue nations that would go to great lengths to get their hands on some easy-to-implement chemical weapon."

"What kinds of weapons are you talking about?"

"We believe the weapons being tested at Bitterroot are a new generation of chemical weapons. Poisonous gases contained in a vial the size of a pencil eraser but capable of killing hundreds in a matter of minutes. We don't know how long it will be before these weapons are fully tested and operational. But you know what could happen if something that deadly fell into the wrong hands."

"If some of the inmates are being killed, what happens to the bodies?"

"Cremation."

Emily wanted desperately to believe he was lying. That he'd made up a fantastic story in order to gain her cooperation. But too much of what he'd told her explained what she'd already suspected.

All she had to do now was figure out what she was going to do about it.

Chapter Six

Zack had never been good at waiting, and riding out the storm was no exception. He cursed the snow as he paced the length of the room for the umpteenth time. Outside the wind continued to rage, battering the old lodge with powerful gusts that shook the walls. A few feet away Emily sat on the bench with her arms wrapped around herself, staring into the fire.

He hadn't liked seeing her go pale when he'd told her what he had discovered about Lockdown, Inc. But her reaction told him two very important things. One, that she believed him. And two, that she wasn't involved. He didn't want to examine too carefully why both of those things pleased him so profoundly.

"What happens next?"

Zack stopped pacing and came over to her side. She looked fragile and feminine sitting on the bench with her chin on her hand, watching him with those cautious whiskey eyes. But while she might be the epitome of feminine beauty, he knew there was nothing fragile about her. What he couldn't explain was why he felt so compelled to protect her. Judging from his track record, Zack figured he was the last man for the job.

"We wait the storm out," he said.

"If what you're saying is true, aren't the people from your agency out looking for us?" she asked impatiently.

"I don't know."

"What do you mean you don't know?"

"I mean there could be a problem."

"What kind of problem?"

Zack said nothing. He didn't quite know how to tell her he couldn't trust the people inside his own agency. He didn't want to believe it himself. But the facts didn't lie.

"Look," she began, "when the visibility improves, this mountain is going to be crawling with men on snowmobiles and skis, not to mention choppers."

"I know," he said. "Damn it."

"So what's your plan?" she asked.

Zack felt like a fool for not having one. But then, he'd assumed he would be able to count on the agency to bail him out if he got into trouble. "I need to get to a phone," he said.

"That's your brilliant plan?" Her laugh grated on his nerves like fingernails scraping down a chalkboard. "I hate to break the news to you, Mr. Secret Agent, but there isn't a phone around for miles."

Temper simmering, he turned to her. "There has to be a ranch or ranger station or something," he said.

"If you're really an agent for some obscure government agency, why can't you call the people you work for?"

Zack hadn't wanted to tell her about the mole. The less she knew about his mission and the agency, the better off she'd be. But thanks to him, she was in this as deep as he was. She deserved to know how serious the situation was because he was starting to wonder if they were going to get out of this alive.

"I think someone at the agency blew my cover," he said hesitantly.

"You mean someone sold you out?"

"It's the only way the people at Lockdown could have found out my identity."

"My God." Her gaze searched his. "Where does that leave us?"

He shook his head, angry that he was in this situation but even angrier because he hadn't seen it coming. "On our own for now."

She took a moment to mull that over. "You mentioned earlier that there are other agents working undercover. Is it possible they're the ones who—"

"No," he said shortly. There was no way fellow agents Kendra Michaels or Jake Vanderpol would have sold him out. He'd known both of them for almost five years. They were two of the best operatives he'd ever known. Good people who would risk their own lives to save a fellow agent.

But Zack knew that if Marcus Underwood was demented enough to test chemical weapons on inmates, he was cruel enough to torture an agent for information. If he'd gotten to Kendra or Jake…

Torture was every agent's worst nightmare. Even though the agents at MIDNIGHT had been trained to endure it, everyone had a breaking point. The thought made him break out in a cold sweat.

Knowing there was nothing he could do until the storm broke, Zack looked at Emily. "How much do you know about Lockdown?" he asked.

"I've been with them for three years. They train their employees and corrections officers well. Their facilities are state of the art."

"So why were you snooping around the infirmary at four o'clock in the morning?"

She looked away, then back at him. "In the last six months, two inmates on my watch disappeared without a trace."

"Are you talking about Big Jimmie Jack and Jinx Ramirez?"

Her eyes widened and she nodded. "One day they were in their cells. The next day the cells were vacant and cleaned. I was trying to find out what happened to them."

"Any luck?"

"All I managed to get were evasive answers."

"Underwood?"

She nodded. "And Dr. Lionel."

"I can fill in at least part of the mystery for you," Zack said. "Big Jimmie Jack went into the infirmary for a sinus infection. Jinx Ramirez went in allegedly for some blood test. Neither man came out. I believe they were murdered."

Emily closed her eyes briefly. "My God."

When her gaze met his, there was a fierceness in its depths he hadn't noticed before. She would be a strong ally—if he could gain her trust. "Anything else?" he asked.

"When I was poking around in the infirmary," she began, "I ran across a file on Signal Research and Development. At the time I didn't think it was significant." Her gaze met his. "Now I'm not so sure."

Zack made the connection immediately. Signal Research and Development was a veterinary pharmaceutical firm. Because of the facility's proximity to the prison, he'd researched it himself, but the company appeared squeaky-clean. Or was it? Had he missed something vital?

"What was in the file?" he asked.

She shook her head. "I wasn't supposed to be there, so I was rushed. I didn't have time to get a good look, but I think there were some invoices."

"Invoices for what?" he asked.

Murder in the name of research.

Neither of them said the words, but Zack could tell by her expression she was thinking the same thing he was.

"You don't think they're somehow involved in chemical weapons research, do you?" she asked.

"I think there are too many coincidences to rule

that out." Coincidences he wished like hell he'd put together before now. "Think about it," he said. "The setup is perfect. Signal is less than five miles from the prison facility. It was built just one year after the Bitterroot prison was built."

"You think this…chemical-weapons-testing project was planned that long ago?"

"I think this operation is more sophisticated than anyone initially envisioned."

And a hell of a lot more dangerous, he silently added. So how was he going to keep this woman safe when he had no way to communicate with the outside world, no transportation and no weapon?

You're going to get her killed the same way you got Alisa killed, a cruel little voice chimed in.

The thought struck him with so much force that Zack flinched, drawing a questioning gaze from Emily. Staring into her pretty eyes, he acknowledged that he did not want the responsibility of her safety on his shoulders. He sure as hell didn't want her blood on his hands.

One woman's death was enough for any man to handle. Zack hadn't handled Alisa's murder well. In the two years since, the guilt had nearly driven him out of his mind. He'd vowed never to put himself in a situation where another person's life—another *woman's* life—was in his hands.

He shouldn't have expected fate to cooperate.

Logic told him to hand Emily over to someone he could trust. An agent at MIDNIGHT or even the local police. But even if he got to a phone and was able to make contact with MIDNIGHT or the local sheriff's department, who could he trust?

Not a soul, that annoying little voice reminded.

"The only thing we can do for now is try getting some rest," he said.

"I have a hard time relaxing when I know there are people out there who want me dead," Emily said.

"You're safe here." *For now.*

"And after the storm breaks?" she asked.

He gave her a hard look. "The moment this storm breaks, I'm going to pay a visit to Signal Research and Development and see if I can figure out what the hell is going on."

EMILY'S MIND WAS TOO troubled to let her sleep. But, overcome with exhaustion, she dozed. And dreamed.

She was back at Bitterroot, lying on an examination table in the infirmary. At the door, Dr. Lionel and Marcus Underwood stood, each of them holding a syringe.

They were going to kill her.

She tried to move only to realize she was strapped securely to the table. She tried to scream, but the terror was like a hand clamped over her throat.

Then Zack Devlin was standing over her. He, too, was holding a syringe. But the intent in the depths of his eyes was different.

"Come with me," he whispered.

His seductive voice glided over her skin like the warm breath of a lover. Her nipples tightened.

"I can't," she said. "You're a convict."

"I'm an undercover agent," he replied. "Let me show you."

Then he was leaning close, and she knew what he would do next. Then his mouth was on hers, and every nerve ending exploded with sensation. His mouth was firm and tantalizing against hers. She tried to resist, but it was as if he'd drugged her and instead she opened to him, taking his tongue into her mouth.

Pleasure crashed over her like a tidal wave. Then his hands were on her body, touching her breasts, the flat plane of her belly, the curve of her hip. Heat flared, and Emily felt herself begin to melt. The need was like a dagger, sharp and endless and danger-ously tempting, and for the first time in her life she knew what it was like to want a man's touch with such desperation that she would cry for it.

She opened to him, wanting, straining to relieve the throbbing arousal between her legs....

"Emily. Hey, it's me, Zack. Wake up."

She jerked awake and opened her eyes to see Zack kneeling over her, his expression concerned. She was lying on her side in front of the hearth with her coat wrapped around her.

A dream, she thought with relief. But the pulse of wet heat between her legs was not her imagina-tion. Neither was the ripple of disappointment that went through her body when she realized Zack Devlin was not kissing her.

"You cried out," he said.

Feeling her cheeks blush, Emily sat up abruptly. "It was just a dream," she said.

He was still kneeling, and she was keenly aware that he was too close. That her body was reacting to his proximity. She saw by the look on his face that if she reached out to him, he would respond.

She couldn't meet his gaze, found herself instead looking at his mouth. That was a mistake because it only made her remember the dream…and the kiss they'd shared back at the prison locker room.

"The storm broke." He rose, and the moment was gone. "In another hour this place is going to be crawling with Lockdown, Inc. people. We need to leave."

Emily scrambled to her feet. "Where are we going?"

"I'm going into Signal Research and Development. I'll find a secure place for you to wait—"

"If you go in, I go in."

"That means if I get caught, so do you," he shot back. "Are you prepared for that?"

"If everything you've told me is true, I want these bastards stopped."

"Emily…"

"I mean it, Zack. I need to do this. I can help. Don't shut me out." She didn't give him a chance to argue. "I'm assuming you have a plan to get in."

"Yeah, it's called winging it."

"Signal Research and Development is a fortress."

"Fortresses are my specialty." Looking nonchalant, he reached into his pocket and withdrew a small bag. "I had room service deliver breakfast while you were sleeping."

The dream she'd been having drifted disturbingly through her mind before she could stop it. Feeling her cheeks heat once again, she looked down at the small bag in his hand. "Chocolate-covered apricots? Where on earth did you get them?"

"I found them in the pocket of this coat." He grinned. "It's not meat and potatoes, but it should get us through the night." He grimaced. "If my calculations are correct, we've got quite a hike ahead of us."

"How far?" she asked.

"Two miles or so. The snow and lack of gear is going to make it tough going." He motioned to her coat, which was still on the floor where she'd been lying. "Let's get out of here before the goons come calling."

MARCUS UNDERWOOD GLARED at Lieutenant Riley Cooper, clenching his hands into fists to keep from doing him physical harm. "You had better have a damn good reason why that chopper is grounded."

"As soon as we're cleared by the FAA, the pilot has been instructed to take her up."

"I want that chopper in the air, Cooper. And I want it in the air yesterday."

"The FAA should give the go-ahead at anytime, Mr. Underwood."

"And meanwhile a dangerous convict and his accomplice are on the loose somewhere in these mountains." Cursing in frustration and fury, he swept his hand toward the wall map. "What other resources are available to us?"

"We've got four snowmobiles."

"Send them out and get me ten more. I want the officers armed and given orders to shoot on sight."

"Sir—"

"Do it, damn it!"

"Yes, sir."

"What else?"

"We've got several ATVs, but they're pretty much useless with all this snow. The mountain roads are impassable."

"Tell me something I don't already know, Cooper."

"We could send a few of our best men out on cross-country skis. We could equip a few with snow-shoes."

"It will be dark soon."

"That won't stop us. We've got night-vision technology."

"Do it now. I don't want any man spared."

"Yes, sir."

Cooper started to turn away, but Underwood reached out, grasped his shoulder and gave it a hard squeeze. "I don't have to tell you what we're up against here, do I, Cooper?"

"I know what's at stake."

"If those two people make it out of these mountains to a phone, if they talk to the wrong person, everything we've worked for goes up in smoke and we could end up spending the rest of our lives in prison. Or worse."

Cooper swallowed hard.

"I want Zack Devlin and Emily Monroe dead before nightfall. By whatever means necessary. Do you understand?"

"I understand."

As the other man walked away, Marcus Underwood wondered if Cooper understood that his life depended on it, too. He'd decided hours ago that if Emily Monroe and Zack Devlin eluded them, Riley Cooper would be the first man to die.

ZACK HAD BEEN RIGHT ABOUT the snow making travel tough. Emily loved the out-of-doors and spent a good bit of her winter leisure time skiing and snowshoeing. But trying to walk through two feet of snow without the proper gear was next to impossible, and within an hour she was exhausted.

"Let's walk to the ridge over there and see if the wind blew most of the snow off the rocks."

She looked over to find Zack watching her. His breaths were puffing out in white clouds of vapor. Even though the temperature was well below freezing, sweat moistened his face. Her only thought was that he didn't look like a convict. That he didn't act like a convict. She wondered if those were the same thoughts that had been running through her father's mind all those years ago when he'd crossed a line....

Zack took her hand. When she tried to loosen his grip, he shot her a sharp look over his shoulder. "It will be easier making it to the top of the rise if you let me help you."

His hand was warm and covered hers completely as he led her up a steep incline. Emily tried hard not to think about how good that warmth felt.

Neither spoke as they made their way to the ridge. The only sound came from the hum of wind coming through the branches and the sound of their boots against the snow. But Emily's mind was in turmoil. Not only was she attracted to this man, but she was beginning to trust him. And trust was a dangerous thing, too.

"Shouldn't be much farther to Signal Research and Development." Zack, who'd let go of her hand and walked a short distance ahead, paused and waited for her to catch up.

Emily couldn't quite meet his gaze as she drew up beside him. "If we manage to get in without getting shot, what exactly are we going to be looking for?"

His mouth tightened. "I don't want you going in with me, Emily. These bastards play for keeps, and I don't want you in the middle of it."

The prospect of facing armed security officers was scary, to say the least. Then she recalled all the men who'd been murdered, and the fear was tempered by a quick jab of determination. "I'm already in the middle of it," she said.

"You're not calling the shots," he snapped.

"I've got as much at stake as you," she shot back.

"You're a civilian. This is my operation."

"I have the right to clear my name!"

He looked as if he would argue, then he glanced away. When he turned back to her, his expression was grim. "If I didn't need your help, there's no way in hell I'd let you do this. Unfortunately for you, I need your help."

"Once we get inside, what are we going to be looking for?" she asked.

"Anything tying Lockdown to Signal. Anything even remotely suspicious."

"I'm assuming you have some brilliant plan that will get us inside."

"I'm working on it."

In the few short minutes they'd stopped to rest, Emily grew chilled. Her hands and feet were numb. The cold stung her cheeks and nose. Zack was standing a couple of feet away. She could just make out his features. His dark eyes. Chiseled mouth. Black slash of his brow. He was watching her. She didn't have a clue what he was thinking or feeling, but she could feel herself responding to him. The memory of the way his mouth had felt against hers stealing into her thoughts…

"You're shivering." Taking a step back, Zack motioned ahead. "Let's keep moving."

Emily was still shaking when she started along the ridge. But the tremors weren't just from the cold. Zack Devlin was affecting her in a way she'd never been affected by another man. Even faced with doing something as dangerous as breaking into a high-security research facility, she couldn't stop thinking about the kiss. She knew it was crazy, but even cold and tired and frightened as she was, the attraction was there, and growing.

"How long have you been an agent with MID-NIGHT?" she asked.

He glanced over at her, his gaze assessing. "Five years."

"You've always been undercover?"

"Deception is my specialty." His smile was self-deprecating. "I'm a good liar."

"I guess you'd have to be to survive a place like Bitterroot for four months."

"It was the longest four months of my life."

Something uncomfortable and all too human flashed in his eyes, and for the first time Emily realized just how brutal such an assignment would have been. She'd been a corrections officer long enough to know what kinds of things went on inside the concrete walls of the prison. Even for a strong man like Zack Devlin the violence and hopelessness would have been formidable.

"It must have been rough," she said.

"I've had better assignments."

"Which cell block were you assigned?"

"2-W."

Because of her gender, she'd never been assigned there, but she knew of 2-W by reputation. It was the cell block where only the most violent and dangerous of offenders were sent. "How did you get assigned to Cell Block 2-W?"

He shot her a wry smile. "I don't know if you've noticed, but I have a smart mouth."

"I've noticed."

He rolled a shoulder. "I mouthed off to the wrong

corrections officer. He saw to it that I got transferred. Then he made it his mission in life to make sure I was as miserable as possible."

The inmates of Cell Block 2-W were only allowed out of their cells for three hours a day. Two or sometimes three men were forced to live in a cramped twelve-by-six-foot cell. The cells were searched for contraband often and without warning and at all times of the day and night. The inmates were routinely taken to the infirmary or shower room and strip-searched for drugs or weapons. Only the most vigorous officers worked Cell Block 2-W. They were the officers who liked their jobs just a little too much. The officers who didn't mind getting into a tussle with a convict. Even if the convict didn't deserve it.

"I couldn't imagine living under those conditions," she said.

"I knew what I was getting into."

"But if what you say about Lockdown, Inc. is true, you could have been killed."

"I'm good at what I do, Emily. MIDNIGHT is careful with their agents." He glanced down at his arm where the GPS device had been removed and laughed. "Besides, the luck of the Irish is in my genes."

"Why did you agree to such an assignment?" she asked.

Zack had asked himself the same question a thousand times in the last four hellish months. Times when he'd been torn from his bunk at three o'clock in the morning and watched while six corrections officers tore apart the cell looking for contraband. Times when he'd been stripped naked and searched if only for the added humiliation.

Zack had never come up with a good answer for why he'd agreed. Maybe because it was his first real mission since Alisa's death. Maybe deep down inside he thought he had something to atone for.

"It's what I do." He said the words after a too-long pause, but he could tell by the expression on Emily's face that she realized there was more to the story. But it was a story Zack didn't want to tell. Especially to a woman whose safety was on his shoulders.

"It seems irresponsible for an agency to send an operative into such a potentially dangerous situation."

"Life is about risk sometimes, Emily. Some of us like it that way. We like it because it makes us feel alive when nothing else even comes close."

At some point they had stopped walking. Zack was facing her. There was just enough light for him to see her features. Her expression was thoughtful and perplexed. He knew the timing couldn't be more wrong, but he liked looking at her. He liked being close to her, talking to her. Even though they were standing in the middle of nowhere about to do something insanely dangerous, he was sorely tempted to take the moment a step further. More than anything, he wanted to lean forward and press his mouth against hers the way he had back at the prison. Even with the armed corrections officer pressing down on them, that taste of her mouth had made him ache in a way he hadn't for a very long time. Made him feel like a man. Like a human being with needs that hadn't been met for what seemed like a lifetime.

"Are you a thrill seeker?" he asked.

"No," she said quickly.

She trembled when he cupped the side of her face with his hand. "Why are you so jumpy?" he whispered.

"I don't like it when you touch me like that."

He couldn't help it. He smiled. "Or maybe you do and you just don't have the guts to admit it."

She started to turn away, but he grasped her arm and unzipped her coat. Before she could stop him, he set his hand just below her left breast, close enough so that he could feel the weight of it against his fingers. "Your heart is pounding, Emily."

"I'm…angry," she said.

"Your pupils are dilated. You're breathing hard." She quivered when he brushed his palm over her breast. Her nipples were hard nubs. He could feel his own body responding. Tightening. His sex growing heavy and uncomfortably full. "You're trembling."

"I'm…cold."

"I don't think the cold is the problem."

"Let go of me."

She started to back away, but he stopped her by grasping her forearms. "Like hell," he growled and lowered his mouth to hers.

Chapter Seven

Emily knew she shouldn't let him kiss her. And for God's sake, she shouldn't be kissing him back! But the hot rush of desire was melting the last of her resolve to do the right thing.

All the while his mouth worked black magic on hers, putting her under a dark spell that only made her want more. She shifted closer so that her body was flush against his. Her coat was open from when he'd unzipped it. Somehow his had come open, too. She could feel the warmth of his body against hers. The hard ridge of his arousal brushing against her belly, which only intensified the hot pulse of her own arousal.

She was aware of her arms going around his neck. Of Zack growling low in his throat. Of his tongue plunging into her mouth to war with hers. Somewhere in the back of her mind a tiny voice told her she was making a mistake.

Abruptly he released her.

She stumbled back, dazed and troubled and damningly aroused. "Don't ever do that again," she said.

"Then don't look at me like you want me to."

They stared at each other for a full minute, their breathing labored and hearts pounding out of control.

Zack then turned away from her and looked out into the vast darkness of the valley below. "I'm sorry. I shouldn't have…done that. I shouldn't have said what I did."

"If we're going to work together and try to figure out what's going on, this can't happen again."

"It won't."

"I have to be able to trust you, Zack."

His eyes glittered as he regarded her, making her feel as if he could look at her and see all the things she didn't want him to see.

"If you're smart, you won't," he said.

The exchange should have cleared the air, but Emily felt more confused than ever. She hated herself for it because her attraction to Zack reminded her too much of the mistakes her father had made.

"We've got about four hours before dawn." Zipping his coat up, he stepped into the darkness. "Let's make some time."

Taking a deep breath, Emily zipped her own coat and fell into place behind him.

ZACK DIDN'T KNOW IF HE was feeling edgy because he was apprehensive about going into Signal Research and Development or because he'd liked kissing Emily and she'd asked him not to do it again. He'd kissed enough women in his time to know when they were enjoying it, and there was no doubt in his mind that Little Miss Corrections Officer had been enjoying that kiss just fine.

He should know better than to get caught up in raw physical attraction. Especially now. He wanted badly to chalk it up to his being stuck in a jail cell for the last four months. But what he felt for Emily was a hell of a lot more complicated than simple attraction. Considering the circumstances, his feelings for her were scaring the hell out of him. Hadn't he learned his lesson with Alisa?

"I see lights."

Emily's voice drew him away from thoughts he had no business brooding over in the minutes before a dangerous operation. Turning, he followed her point. Sure enough, he could see the glow of lights in the valley below.

He recalled from the map that Signal Research and Development sat on about sixty wooded acres. Since the facility hadn't been under suspicion, he'd given it only a cursory look. Now that he needed to get inside, he sorely wished he'd taken the time to study the layout more thoroughly.

"How much do you know about this place?" he asked.

"Very little, unfortunately. The company is low-key. They make pharmaceutical drugs and supplies for veterinarians. They employ quite a few people in the area. I've driven by a few times. They have pretty good security, including a chain-link fence with barbed wire and lots of lighting."

"Swell."

They were standing behind an outcropping of rock, and Emily was gazing down at the facility below. Zack should have been assessing the compound, but his attention was irresistibly drawn to Emily. Her face was lovely in the dim light filtering down from a crescent moon. Her cheeks were blushed with cold, and she looked excited and scared at once. Maybe he wasn't the only one who got off on risk.

He forced himself to tear his gaze away from her and study the complex instead. There were three buildings, each a two-story brick with a sloping roof. Windows were sparse. The entrances were well lit.

"Someone is definitely concerned with security," he said, wishing for a set of blueprints.

"How do we get in?"

"If it was daylight, we could wait for a delivery truck, overpower the driver or stow away in the truck." He glanced over at her. "But it's three in the morning. I doubt they're going to be receiving many deliveries at this hour."

"Maybe we can find a place away from those lights, cut the fence and go in that way."

He shook his head. "Too risky." But the mention of lights sparked another idea. "We cut the power."

"How do you propose we do that?"

He surveyed the line of telephone poles that ran the length of the paved roadway leading to the parking lot. "See those telephone poles? They support the power lines to the entire facility. If we can down one of the poles, that should take out the power."

"Let's do it." Emily started to rise, but he snagged her coat and held her back.

"The bad news is they probably have a backup generator," he said.

"Oh."

"The good news is it will probably take a few minutes for the backup power to kick on."

She bit her lip. "We'll just have to move quickly."

Frowning because he didn't like the enthusiasm in her voice, he turned to her—and immediately wished he hadn't. She was looking straight at him, not the facility. She looked soft and lovely and he wanted nothing more than to sink his hands into her warmth and forget all about Lockdown, Inc. and Signal Research and Development.

"You sure you're up to this?" he asked.

"No," she said. "But I don't think I have a choice."

"You could stay here and wait for me."

"I've never been very good at waiting."

Unable to stop himself, Zack reached over and touched her cheek with the back of his hand. Her skin was cool and incredibly soft beneath his knuckles. "You keep impressing me, Emily."

"And you're a smooth-talking con." She swatted his hand away.

He smiled. "Don't let the accent fool you. There's

nothing smooth about me. I'm as rough around the edges as a man can get. You'd be wise to remember that."

Realizing he was letting himself get distracted, Zack moved away from her and turned his attention to the facility.

"How long will we have before backup lighting comes on?" she asked.

"If it's a flywheel assembly, backup power will be instantaneous. If it's diesel-powered, it will take a few minutes. With a campus this size, I'm betting the backup power generates light for only the areas vital to operation. Refrigeration. Computers. Emergency and security lighting. That sort of thing. This is graveyard shift. They're probably working with a skeleton crew. That will be a plus."

"How long will we have once we're inside?"

He looked at her and found himself wishing he'd never involved her. A suicide mission wasn't the sort of operation in which to involve a civilian. Particularly a woman he was attracted to....

"Fifteen minutes," he said. "Twenty max. Whatever the case, we'll need to act quickly."

He only hoped it would be fast enough to get them out alive.

EMILY'S ENTIRE BODY WAS zinging with adrenaline as they sprinted across the snow-covered field toward the twelve-foot-high chain-link fence. Back when she'd been safely ensconced behind the rocks and hidden by darkness, breaking into Signal Research and Development had seemed like a good idea. Now that she and Zack were in open view, she questioned the wisdom of her decision to accompany him.

What the hell had she been *thinking?* She barely knew Zack Devlin and yet here she was risking her life. Then there was the little problem of her burgeoning attraction to him. And that blasted kiss. Well, two kisses to be exact. Maybe she had finally gone around the bend.

When they reached the fence, it took all of two seconds for Emily to see that getting onto the grounds was going to be trickier than they'd expected. A few feet away Zack was already at the fence, kneeling, opening the satchel tied to his belt.

"How are we going to get over triple strands of barbed wire and not come out of this looking like raw hamburger?"

Glancing over his shoulder, Zack pulled some type of tool from the bag.

"What is that?" she asked.

"The kind of Swiss Army knife that would get a civilian thrown into jail if he brought it to show-and-tell." He pressed a button on the handle and a nasty-looking blade swished into view.

Emily studied the small, compact blade. "You expect a knife to cut through chain fencing?"

"This titanium blade will make short work of that fence." Putting the blade to the first link, he went to work sawing. "Observe."

The first wire snapped almost instantly. In two

minutes he'd snipped enough strands to create a big hole that the both of them could squeeze through. "Any questions?"

"You mean aside from the little voice inside my head asking me if I'm totally nuts?"

Grinning, he rose to his full height. "We've all got that little voice inside our heads, Emily. The key is learning when to listen and when to shut it out."

"Even when it's right?"

"Especially when it's right." He took her hand. "Come on."

They squeezed through the fence. Then, using the shadows of the pines that grew along the perimeter of the property as cover, they went into a sprint. A hundred yards away she spotted the parking lot. Several cars and trucks were parked close to the main building. An asphalt driveway streaked north toward the main road where a small guard shack stood.

Zack went into the shadows and stopped twenty yards from the roadway. Emily was breathing hard and sweating. Less than a foot away, Zack was looking at her with dark, dangerous eyes.

"Did you see the snowplow next to the outbuilding?" he asked.

"I saw it. Right next to the red SUV with the dented fender." She could hear the rumble of its engine. The smell of diesel fuel filling the air. "What are we going to do? Clear the driveway for them?"

He smiled, but it looked forced. He was obviously every bit as apprehensive about this as she was. "We're going to use the plow to down a tele-phone pole and take out the electricity."

It was as good an idea as they were going to come up with. If they caught a break, Emily thought as they started toward the plow, they might just pull it off without getting shot.

Chapter Eight

Emily couldn't believe she was doing this. Risking everything—her career, her reputation, her very life—on the word of a man she had every reason not to trust. Or did she?

Halfway to the snowplow, she noticed a man standing a few feet from the massive vehicle's blade. He was facing away from them, relieving himself, of all things. Had she not been quite so terrified she might have laughed. But Emily had been in enough dangerous situations in her life to appreciate just how bad this could get.

Zack turned to her, his gaze seeking hers. He put his finger to his lips, then motioned for her to stay put. She nodded and watched as he approached the man alone, his stride confident, as if he had every right in the world to be there. Emily hoped the man wasn't armed.

"Got a light?"

The man started, quickly shook himself, zipped and turned. He was heavyset and wearing insulated coveralls over a hooded sweatshirt. "Who the hell are you?" he asked.

"Your replacement," Zack said amicably.

"Replacement?" The man made an unflattering reference to Zack's mother. "This is a secure facility. What are you doing here?"

"I was wondering if I could borrow your snowplow for a few minutes."

The man's sneer disappeared. His eyes widened. Then he reached for something clipped to his belt. Zack moved so quickly, the man didn't even see it coming. One moment he was putting his radio to his mouth, the next he was dropping like a three-hundred-pound rag doll. Zack was almost to the plow by the time the other man hit the ground.

"What did you do to him?" Emily asked.

"I taught him what happens to big-mouthed idiots when they say unflattering things about me mum." Stepping onto the big tractor plow, he tossed her a coil of rope. "Tie him up, will you?"

Emily caught the rope with one hand. "Okay."

Zack settled onto the seat and rammed the shifter into place. The gears ground for an instant, then the big plow jumped forward. "This shouldn't take long."

It wasn't easy tying the hands of a three-hundred-pound unconscious man. It took every bit of her strength just to roll him onto his stomach. Her hands shook as she wrapped the rope around his wrists and knotted it. She'd barely finished when a crash behind her sent her a foot into the air.

She turned in time to see the plow blade crash into the telephone pole. Wood splintered. A streak of blue electricity arced through the sky. She smelled burning rubber. She watched as Zack slid from the plow and came running toward her.

"Nice job," she said.

"Thanks." He looked down at the man. "Let me hide porky here and we'll be on our way." Stooping, he picked up the man's torso by the shoulders and began dragging him to some nearby bushes. "Best to keep him out of sight for now." He plucked the man's security badge from his shirt and the flashlight from his belt and stuffed both into his coat pocket. "These might come in handy."

A giddy laugh that was part terror, part utter disbelief jammed in her throat. She couldn't believe she was about to break into a pharmaceutical firm to look for clues in a mystery that was as unbelievable as the plot of some cheesy thriller.

Zack came up beside her then and tilted his head as if to look closely at her. A tuft of hair had fallen onto his forehead. He was looking at her intently. "You've got about five seconds to change your mind about this."

She shook her head adamantly. "Let's go find what we need to bring down those bastards at Lockdown."

One side of his mouth curved. "That's the spirit," he said and took her hand. "Let's see how good we are at breaking and entering."

The downing of the telephone pole had taken out

all lights except for a few exterior security lights powered by the generator, which had kicked on automatically. Zack gripped her hand as he led her across the tarmac toward the rear of the main building. Two men ran out the double doors, pulling on coats and equipment. Zack hauled Emily behind a Dumpster just before they would have been spotted. Forcing her to kneel, he dropped to his knees beside her and put his arms around her only to discover that she was trembling.

Putting his mouth close to her ear, he breathed in her scent and found himself wishing he'd met her under different circumstances. "Easy," he whispered. "I'm not going to let anything happen to you."

Silly words, considering. *Not to mention your track record,* a cruel little voice added.

He held Emily for a minute. Once the two men were out of earshot, he turned her to him. Her eyes were wide. Her mouth wet and full. Her nostrils flaring with every exhalation. Her face was pale, but the cold had turned her cheeks rosy. He'd never seen a more beautiful woman in his entire life.

Zack leaned forward and brushed his mouth against hers. She didn't resist. But she didn't kiss him back, either. Zack didn't care. After that first dangerous contact, all he wanted was more.

Her lips were sweet and soft and wet against his. He wanted badly to deepen the kiss, but some shred of logic held him back. He pulled away, as stunned by his response to her as by the fact that he could be so foolish as to get caught up in a kiss at a time like this.

She was looking at him as if to ask, *Why did you do that?*

"Every man has his limit," he said. "Including me."

"I'll try to remember that," she said dazedly.

Taking her hand, he helped her to her feet. "Let's go."

Using the plow driver's security access card, they entered the main building through the rear door. The interior was dark and smelled of floor wax, heated air and paper dust. Zack's eyes slowly adjusted to the near total darkness. They were standing in a small nondescript foyer with a reception window, a red leather sofa and two matching chairs and a coffee table piled with magazines.

Never releasing Emily's hand, he crossed to the only door and swiped the security badge through the reader. The lock clicked and he shoved open the door.

"Where are we going?" Emily whispered.

"Let's see if we can find a file room or maybe some of the offices."

"Devlin, this is such a long shot."

"I know," he muttered, annoyed because she was right. Because he didn't have a better plan. Damn it. He turned to her. "If we get caught, I want you to tell them I've been holding you hostage."

She stared at him, her eyes large and fragile in the dim light. "But you haven't—"

"This is no time for loyalty to me," he said. "These people have a lot at stake and they're playing for keeps. If you want to live, tell them I forced you into this."

"What about you?"

"I do this for a living, remember?" When she only continued to stare at him, he added, "I've got MIDNIGHT to back me. I'll be fine."

Still, Zack doubted either of them would survive if they were caught. And not for the first time he mentally kicked himself for involving her. "Come on," he said. "We don't have much time."

A single yellow light illuminated the hall just enough for him to make out the signs on the doors. In the distance he could hear the occasional door slamming, telling him there were people in the building, moving around, probably wondering what had happened to the power. Twice he and Emily had to duck into an alcove to miss being seen. Once by a woman with a flashlight. And then by two security officers toting guns. If it hadn't been so dark, they would have been caught red-handed….

"What were those two men doing with guns in a veterinary pharmaceutical firm?" Emily whispered as they stepped back into the hall.

"I'll bet the farm this place doesn't have a damn thing to do with veterinary medicine." *And everything to do with chemical weapons and Lockdown, Inc.,* he thought darkly.

They passed an elevator. The bell dinged, warning them of the arrival of someone else on the floor.

"Damn, this place is busy at this hour," Zack muttered. Grabbing Emily's arm, he darted toward an Exit sign at the end of the hall. He pushed open the door, and they slipped into the darkened stairwell just as two men stepped off the elevator.

"That was close," he said.

"Too close. How are we going to find what we're looking for?" She was breathing hard. Even in the darkness, Zack could see that she was an inch away from panic. "We don't even know where to begin."

"Take it easy, Emily."

"Take it easy? This place is crawling with men toting guns and you're telling me to take it easy?"

Zack didn't like seeing her so shaken. He sure didn't like seeing her afraid. Not tough-talking Emily Monroe who'd been ready, willing and damn near able to take him down when he'd accosted her in the Bitterroot infirmary.

"Nobody knows we're here yet," he said. "We've got a few minutes. Let's use those minutes wisely, see what we can find, then we'll get the hell out of Dodge, okay?"

A breath shuddered out of her, then she nodded. "Okay."

He motioned toward the stairs he assumed would take them to the basement. "I'm betting the file room is in the basement."

"How do you know that?"

"People like window offices."

They took the steps two at a time, their boots nearly silent on the concrete. The basement was quiet and cold and dark. A single red Exit light shone at the end of a long hall. "I'll take the doors on the right," Zack whispered. "You take the ones on the left. If you find one unlocked, let me know and we'll go in together."

Emily nodded and they went to work. Zack was almost all the way down the hall and thinking the entire operation was going to be a bust when the knob he tried twisted and the door swung open. "I'm in," he said, then walked inside.

The room was large, with low ceilings and crowded with file cabinets of all shapes and sizes. Tiny ground-level windows offered stingy light from outside. It would have to do. The first file cabinet Zack tried was locked. Frustration burned through him. He tried another, found it locked, as well. Cursing beneath his breath, he looked around for something to break the locking mechanism with.

"I think I found something."

He glanced over to see Emily leaning over a battered desk piled high with brown expandable folders. A plastic sign on the in-box read: To Be Filed. Zack felt a grin emerge. Even companies with something to hide had file clerks that didn't get all their work finished by the end of the day.

He crossed to the desk. Emily had emptied a folder onto its scarred wooden surface and was looking through papers. "This one was labeled Lockdown, Inc.," she said.

Excitement coursed through Zack as he pulled the flashlight from his coat and shone it on the file.

After reaching dead end after dead end, he had thought the excursion hopeless. Hopefully this would prove him wrong.

"Looks like someone's notes. Some scientist or researcher." Emily lowered herself into the desk chair. "They're in order by the date in the upper right-hand corner of the page. See?"

"Keep going." Zack's heart had begun to pound.

"They mention 'mortality rate' here." She set her finger against the handwritten notes. "'Subcutaneous hemorrhage. Severe irritation of mucous membranes.'"

"Hell."

"What's RZ-902?"

At the mention of RZ-902, Zack could feel sweat breaking out beneath his arms. "I believe you just found what we were looking for."

Nudging her aside, he looked down at the notes and began to read. Dread built inside him at the words scrawled on the page.

The testing phase of RZ-902 is more successful than planned. Mortality rate stands at 98.1 percent. Fatal outcome from the moment of introduction is 4.2 minutes. It is the opinion of the study that RZ-902 is ready for mass production, the first phase of which will take less than two weeks, depending on delivery of supplies. The final product will be ready for market by the end of the month.

Zack almost couldn't comprehend what he was reading. He'd seen a lot of horrific things in the years he'd worked for MIDNIGHT. He'd met more

than his share of ruthless human beings, men and
women who would stoop to any level for money or
power or some combination of the two. But in all his
years of working undercover he'd never encountered true evil.

Until now.

"Zack, what is it?"

He didn't even realize he was leaning heavily
against the desk. That he was breathing heavily. And
shaken to his core. He raised his gaze to Emily's. He
wondered how such a good woman could be tangled
up in such a god-awful mess. Then he remembered
he was the one who'd dragged her into this. That
now it was up to him to keep her safe.

The same way you kept Alisa safe?

"We've got to get out of here," he said.

"What are you talking about? We've just found
what we've been looking—"

"Don't ask any more questions. Let's go."

"Zack, you're scaring me."

Without looking at her or speaking he began gathering the papers as quickly as he could, grabbing the
ones he thought would be most useful, leaving the
rest.

"My God, you're shaking." She touched his arm,
drawing his gaze. "Talk to me? What is this?"

"RZ-902," he said, grinding out the words.
"They've finished the testing. Weeks ahead of sched-
ule."

"What does that mean exactly?"

"That means that Lockdown, Inc. and Signal Research and Development stand to make a hell of a lot of money from anyone willing to pay the price. Terrorists. Dictators. Any demented son of a bitch who wants to wipe out a city anywhere in the world will be able to do that if he gets his hands on this poison."

"My God." She blanched. "What do we do now?"

"I'm going to grab as many of these notes as I can carry, then we've got to get you out of here."

"Zack, we have to stop this. I'm not leaving until—"

In an instant he had her against the desk, his hands wrapped around her arms, his face inches from hers. "You're not going to do a damn thing. This is my mission. My problem. As of now you're out of it."

"I'm going to finish this."

"We're going to walk out of here, then I'm taking you to the police."

"How do you know the police aren't in on this?"

Zack stared at her, knowing he was making a fatal mistake. Knowing he was acting on emotion and not the logic he'd always prided himself on possessing. He knew he couldn't turn her over to the police. What he needed to do was contact MIDNIGHT and figure out who the mole was. He could no longer handle this on his own. He needed the agency's help. But first they had to get the hell out of this godforsaken facility.

Feeling frustrated and more frightened than he

wanted to admit, Zack released her, then looked down at the papers spread out on the desk. "Damn it."

Emily reached for the papers, but Zack stopped her. He knew it was stupid, but he didn't want her touching anything even remotely related to RZ-902. If they got caught, her only hope of coming out of this alive was if she convinced them Zack had taken her hostage.

He was in the process of stuffing the papers into the waistband of his trousers when, without warning, the door to the office swung open. Zack caught a glimpse of a male silhouette. The beam of a flashlight. Soundlessly he moved toward Emily, wrapped his arms around her and took her down to the floor.

"Don't make a sound," he whispered.

"Who's there?" a male voice called out. "Show yourselves or I'm going to start shooting."

He was so close to Emily, he could feel the rapid rise and fall of her chest, the warmth of her breath on his cheek. He sensed the fear coming off her. She was beginning to hyperventilate. If her breathing got any louder, the man would surely hear her....

The flashlight beam skimmed over the top of the desk, which was the only thing keeping them from certain discovery.

"What now?" she whispered.

"I believe the scientific term for it is *running*." Pulling back slightly, he gave her a smile. "On my cue we're going to run for the door."

"What cue?"

"You'll know." He couldn't manage a smile this

time. The tension was tightening around his body like a knot. If anything happened to this woman, he would never forgive himself.

Taking one last look at her face, he shifted slightly, shoved his hand into the satchel at his belt and took out his remaining concussion grenade. He'd been saving it as a last resort for an emergency situation. He figured this qualified.

Never taking his eyes from hers, he pulled the clip, silently counted to three, then tossed it in the general direction of the man's voice. The grenade hit the floor with a dull thud and rolled.

"What the hell is—"

The blast shook the room, temporarily deafening him. Smoke billowed, pitching them into complete darkness. Zack jumped up and pulled Emily to her feet. "Run!" he commanded.

Zack and Emily streaked across the room and burst into the hall. Dim light and fresh air met them. Zack's ears were ringing, but he could still hear shouting coming from down the hall. Flashlight beams slashed through the darkness. His fear notched up when he realized a group of men had heard the blast and were approaching at a very fast pace.

"This way!" he whispered and pulled her back into the room.

Once inside, he turned and locked the door. The grenade had done its job, filling the room with thick black smoke. The man stumbled about, bumping into furniture. "Who's there?" he shouted.

Then a single gunshot split the air. Cursing, Zack

shoved Emily in the general direction of the farthest window. There was no way the man could see them. But he could get off a lucky shot.

"What are you *doing?*" Emily cried when they reached the window.

"You're going out that window." Not waiting for a response, Zack picked up a nearby stool and shattered the glass. "Go!" Lifting her, praying she could avoid any glass he'd missed, he shoved her toward the window.

Small-framed, she wriggled through the opening with relative ease. Once she was through, Zack stepped onto the stool. Behind him he could hear pounding on the door. Shouts coming from the hall. He knew the security personnel were equipped with radios. It would only be a matter of seconds before they realized their mysterious intruders had slipped out of the building.

Zack forced his body through the window, the glass breaking beneath his weight, the sharp edges scraping against the fabric of his coat. He felt a shard pierce his left hand, but the pain barely registered over his growling fear. If he got stuck, both of them were as good as dead.

Then he was through the window, on his hands and knees in the snow. The night embraced him like a cold but dear friend.

"Oh, my God. You're bleeding."

Zack looked down to see blood dripping from his hand. "As long as it's not from a bullet, I'm not going to worry about it." Scrambling quickly to his feet, he scanned the area. They'd come out on the west side of the building. Twenty yards away two four-wheel-drive vehicles sat rumbling in the parking lot, exhaust billowing into the frigid night air.

"We need a vehicle," he said.

"I don't think we're going to—"

Emily's words were cut off when a bullet slammed into the brick less than a foot from where she was standing. Zack heard her yelp. He saw her hand shoot up to her cheek. Worry tore through him when he saw blood, thought she'd been shot.

"Emily!"

"I'm...okay," she said. "Piece of brick caught me."

Zack looked over his shoulder to see the spotlight mounted on the rear of one of the four-wheel-drive trucks sweep toward them. There was no time to steal a vehicle.

Taking Emily's hand, he pulled her into a dead run toward the hole he'd cut earlier in the fence.

If their luck held, they might just make it out alive.

Chapter Nine

Emily ran as she had never run before. She ran until her legs burned. Until she thought her lungs would burst into flames. Just when she thought she could go no farther, another wave of adrenaline pumped her forward. They ran over fields blanketed with deep snow. Through forests dense with trees and brush. Down ravines riddled with loose rock. Over ice and through fast-moving water.

Emily ran until her body literally gave out. In a small gully filled with sapling pine her legs tangled, and she was flung facedown into two feet of snow.

For several long seconds all she could do was suck oxygen into her burning lungs. She saw Zack collapsing onto the snow beside her, heard his heavy breathing punctuated by the frenzied pound of her own heart.

Slowly their breathing began to regulate and she became aware of the sound of rushing water in the distance. Of an owl hooting from a tree. The wind turning the winter branches into bony fingers reaching for a black sky. Of Zack rising, grumbling as he brushed the snow from his coat and pants.

Emily rolled over and struggled shakily to her feet. "If I live through this, I'm not going to have to go to the gym for a month."

Zack's gaze met hers. He wasn't smiling. In fact, he looked as downtrodden as she'd ever seen him.

"What's wrong?" she asked.

"I dropped the papers. The notes." Cursing viciously, he slapped some more snow from his coat. "I had them in my hand, but when that bastard started shooting…" Shaking his head angrily, he set his hand against a nearby tree and leaned. "*Damn it.*"

Emily knew it was pointless to get angry. But she was exhausted and cold and more frightened than she'd ever been in her life. Before realizing she was going to move, she was across the snow and jamming her finger into his chest.

"You mean to tell me we went in there for nothing?"

"That's exactly what I'm telling you."

She couldn't believe it. She could feel her frustration building. "And you call yourself an agent? How could you do something so…unprofessional?"

"I was a little busy getting shot at." Shoving his hands into his pockets, he turned away from her abruptly and walked several feet away. Emily could see his breaths puffing out into the frigid night air and understood how much this had upset him. Guilt nipped at her.

"I'm sorry," she said. "I shouldn't have blamed you. I didn't mean to upset you."

"You didn't," he snapped, turning back to her.

But she could tell by the tight set of his jaw and the dark flash of his eyes that she had. And not just a little. Zack Devlin was as upset as a man could be.

"I can't believe I bloody screwed this up," he said.

"Those weren't the best of circumstances back there."

His jaw flexed. "I just about got you killed."

"No." She pointed toward the direction from which they'd come. "The people at Signal and the bastards at Lockdown are the ones to blame for this. Not you."

"I dragged you into this."

"I hate to refute your preconceived notions about me, but I have a mind of my own, Devlin. I'm the one who made the decision to go in there with you."

He regarded her thoughtfully for a moment. "Yeah, well, thanks for letting me off the hook."

"I don't think either of us is off the hook just yet."

Realizing she was right, that they were wasting precious time, he looked around at their surroundings. "We need to keep moving."

"Where do we go?"

"Someplace where we can rest, get some sleep and food," he said. "How well do you know this area?"

"Well enough to know there's not a soul who will rent rooms to two people whose photos have been flashed on every television station in the county."

"Is there a motel in the vicinity?"

"There's a bed-and-breakfast near the state park." Sighing, she looked around. "I'm not exactly sure where we are, but it's only a few miles down the road from Signal Research and Development."

"It can't be far."

Her gaze met Zack's. "We can't just walk in and check in. The desk clerk will recognize us and have every cop in the county knocking on our door before we can kick off our boots."

A bit of the old humor came back into his eyes. "Don't be so sure about that."

She watched as he untied the satchel from his belt. Sinking into the snow, he opened the bag and removed several items. "What are you doing?" she asked.

"Becoming someone else."

She watched him dab something onto his palms and slick back his hair. Using the same gel-type substance, he adhered a thin black mustache to his upper lip. Next came the heavy, dark-framed eyeglasses. A clip-on tie.

"My God," she said. "A disguise."

"Any self-respecting agent has a quick-change disguise." Shooting her a smile, he pulled a tube from the satchel and squeezed a small amount onto his palm. "I might need your help with this one."

Emily crossed to him and knelt. "What is it?"

"Culloden." When she only continued to stare questioningly at him, he added. "It's similar to wax. Dries quickly. Perfect for scars."

He expertly applied the substance to the outside corner of his right eye. Within minutes he had formed a perfect scar.

"How do I look?" he asked, getting to his feet.

Emily couldn't take her eyes off him. In less than two minutes he'd gone from rough-around-the-edges inmate to nerdy bookworm fresh from some dusty bookstore. "You really are an agent," she whispered.

He grinned. "Just wait until you see my Johnny Depp impersonation."

THE LOST CANYON Bed-and-Breakfast was located in a small town not far from the Salmon River. Emily and Zack traveled most of the way via a small frozen creek, their footprints obscured by high grass, jutting rock and sometimes swiftly moving water. Twice they had to take cover when men on snowmobiles edged dangerously close. Both times they'd barely avoided being spotted.

Zack couldn't remember the last time he'd been so utterly exhausted. His feet were wet and numb. His hands ached with cold and he felt frozen all the way to his bones. He could only imagine how Emily must feel.

"Nice place," he commented as they approached the rustic grouping of cabins from the rear.

"I wonder if they've already been here looking for us," she said.

"I'm sure they have." He looked over at her and grimaced. She looked near collapse, if he wanted to be honest about it. Damn, he hated putting her through this. He'd originally planned to disguise Emily, as well, and check in as husband and wife, but he wasn't sure she had the energy left to do it.

Stopping at a picnic table beneath a stand of ponderosa pines, he turned to her. "I want you to wait here while I check in."

She collapsed onto the bench. "They'll recognize that coat you're wearing."

He glanced down at the coat. Criminy, he'd nearly forgotten. "I must be getting sloppy." Quickly he removed the satchel from his belt and pulled out the phony trench coat. It was made of a special fabric that compressed exponentially but never wrinkled. With a single shake he had a full-length trench coat—less the bulk.

"How do I look?" he asked, slipping it onto his shoulders.

"Like a vacuum-cleaner salesman."

He grinned. "I was going for antiquarian-book connoisseur, but door-to-door salesman will do just fine." He leaned close and brushed his lips against hers. Even though the contact was light, he felt it like a jolt of electricity charging through his body. Her lips were soft and warm despite the cold, and for an instant Zack thought he was going to fall right into the kiss….

Her expression was startled when he pulled back. "What was that for?" she asked.

"Luck," he said and headed toward the bed-and-breakfast office.

The pleasure of the kiss was still vibrating through him when he opened the door and stepped into the small, cluttered office. The place was overheated and smelled of dust. In the corner a television was blaring a local newscast. The clerk behind the counter was leaning back in his chair, asleep.

Zack walked up to the counter and hit the bell with his palm. The clerk jerked awake, his feet hitting the floor at the same time his eyes opened. "Didn't hear you come in."

"Sorry to wake you," Zack said, using his best East Coast inflection. "Do you have a room?"

The kid stood and walked to the counter, stretching. "We got one cabin left."

"That'll do."

The kid slid a form across the counter. "Fill this out."

"Certainly." Zack set his phony wallet on the counter, then set to work filling out the form with false information.

"Where you headed?" the clerk asked.

"Convention in Boise." Because he didn't want to partake in idle chat, he quickly finished the form and fished several bills from his wallet. "What time is checkout?"

"Noon."

Zack looked at the cuckoo clock on the wall. That would give them a few hours to shower and sleep. After that he wasn't sure what to do. Maybe after he got some rest he would be able to think straight.

After all, he was working on thirty-six hours with no sleep and very little to eat.

At the door he stopped and turned to the clerk. "What are the chances of my getting some food?"

"Not good," the clerk said.

Zack crossed back to the counter, dug a twenty-dollar bill from the wallet and laid it on the wood surface. "You sure about that?"

The clerk's eyes widened. "I've got a hot plate in the closet. I could probably dig up some soup."

"I'll wait."

Two minutes later Zack left the office with a hot plate and a family-size can of vegetable soup in tow. It wasn't much, but it would sustain them until they could get a decent meal the next day.

It seemed as if the temperature had dropped twenty degrees in the few minutes he'd been inside. He glanced across the snow-covered parking lot toward the picnic table where he'd left Emily. A chill passed through him when he found the table empty.

Where the hell was she?

He crossed the small lot at full speed. At the picnic table he slid to a stop—and froze. She was curled on the bench, asleep. Relief made his legs go weak. She was lying on her side with her arms wrapped around her body, so beautiful it hurt just to look at her. And an emotion that was part affection, part something he didn't want to acknowledge, went through him.

Setting the soup and hot plate on the table, he bent and scooped her into his arms. Her eyes fluttered, widened.

"It's just me," Zack whispered.

She looked around quickly, as if trying to orient herself. "What—"

"You fell asleep."

"I just closed my eyes for a second."

"It's all right." He bent slightly toward the bench. "Grab that hot plate and can of soup, will you?"

"You can put me down, you know. I can walk."

"You're wiped out."

She didn't protest when he turned and started toward cabin number six. Nestled amongst a few winter-dead cottonwood trees at the rear, the cabin was relatively private, out of sight from the road and the office.

On the wooden porch Emily slid from his arms and Zack unlocked the door. The single-room cabin was rustic, with a corner woodstove, pine-plank floors and rough-hewn cedar beams. A small iron bed dressed in a white down comforter and several Southwestern-themed throw pillows dominated the room. A door to the left opened to a small bathroom with a stand-up shower. A sliding door to the right revealed a postage-stamp-size closet.

"Home, sweet home," Zack said, switching on the light and stepping into the room.

Emily came up beside him. "Not exactly the Hilton, but it will do in a pinch."

He watched her carry the hot plate to the table by the single window. Zack knew his mind should be on how he was going to get them out of this mess. On how he was going to find the mole at MID-

NIGHT while at the same time eluding the people from Lockdown and Signal Research and Development. But watching Emily, he found he couldn't think about anything except the way she moved, the radiance of her face, the way she'd tasted when he'd kissed her.

He walked up beside her and eased the hot plate from her hand. "Let me take care of that."

"If I stop moving, I'll collapse," she said.

"That's the idea," he said. "Take a shower. I'll warm the soup. Then we'll get some sleep."

"Are you forgetting there are people with guns looking for us?"

He hadn't forgotten that. Not by a long shot. But Zack knew what exhaustion and hunger could do to a person. It could wear them down, weaken them, not only physically but psychologically, too. "We'll grab a couple of hours of sleep, some food, then we'll see if we can come up with a plan."

If he only had an idea of what that might be.

THE MAN IN THE SUIT COULDN'T believe the situation had deteriorated so severely and so rapidly. There were too many people involved, and all of them were asking questions. Questions he didn't have a clue how to answer.

A knock sounded at his door. *About time,* he thought. "It's open," he snapped from behind his desk.

The man who entered the office walked with a limp and carried a thin portfolio. Without speaking, he took the chair opposite the desk and set the portfolio on the glossy surface.

"Devlin's file?" The man opened the portfolio. His mouth stretched into a smile as he began to read. "Excellent," he said, aware that his heart was beating quickly. But it was from excitement this time, not fear or dread or all the things he'd been feeling since Devlin and Emily Monroe had fled Bitterroot some thirty-six hours earlier.

When he'd finished reading, he put his hands behind his head and leaned back in his chair. "Devlin has quite an interesting history, doesn't he?"

"He definitely has a weak link."

He reached for the phone on his desk and punched in a two-digit speed dial. "I want you to put together a file on Emily Monroe. I want to know everything there is to know about her. I want this information yesterday. Do you understand?" He smiled at the voice on the other end. "Excellent."

A knock at the door drew both men's attention. "Come in," the man behind the desk said.

Marcus Underwood walked in. "You wanted to see me?"

"Sit down."

Underwood took a seat in the second visitor's chair and tried not to act nervous. But his forehead was slick with sweat.

"Have you contained the problem yet?" the man behind the desk asked.

Underwood shifted in the chair. "Not yet."

Turning slightly, the man swiveled in his chair

and looked out at the predawn darkness. Devlin and the Monroe woman were still out there somewhere. Roaming free and carrying secrets that would destroy everything he'd worked for if those secrets were leaked to the wrong person. God in heaven, how could this have happened?

He turned his attention back to Underwood. "I want every man and woman we've got working on this Devlin thing. Do you understand?"

"We've got over thirty men working a twenty-mile perimeter."

"Then why the hell haven't you found them!" he exploded.

The prison administrator licked his lips, looked nervously from the man sitting next to him to the man behind the desk. "Devlin has proven himself quite resourceful."

"You have every resource at your fingertips," the man behind the desk said in a low, dangerous voice. "Use them. Find that son of a bitch and his accomplice."

"I'll do my best."

He thought about it some more, felt another squeeze of panic. "If we don't find them by noon today, we're going to have to bring in law enforcement."

The man in the wingback chair spoke for the first time since Underwood entered the room. "If Devlin or Monroe talk to the wrong cop, it could present an even more complicated problem. Devlin can be quite convincing."

"We'll just have to make sure that doesn't happen, won't we?"

"How do you propose to do that?"

"Let me spell it out for both of you." The man behind the desk looked at Underwood. "Put out a press release to the local media. Do what you have to do to discredit Emily Monroe. Leak the photo of her and Devlin kissing in the locker room. Doctor it if you have to, but make it persuasive and compelling. Make sure Lockdown, Inc. sounds reliable and trustworthy. But make damn sure she is portrayed as his accomplice. Make sure you mention her father."

"Consider it done."

The man in the wingback chair smiled. "Damn, you're cold-blooded."

The man behind the desk leaned back in his executive chair and studied the two men before him. "Once word is out that there has been a jailbreak, that an Irish terrorist had inside help, that he is armed and dangerous, killing them shouldn't be a problem."

"What if local law enforcement nabs them first?"

"You had better make sure that doesn't happen. I want them dead before they do any damage to the RZ-902 program. Make sure Devlin gets the blame for killing the woman. We don't need any more complications."

"I understand."

"Make sure you do." He glanced at the file he'd just read. "If all else fails and you can't get to Devlin, get the woman and bring her to me. Devlin will follow." He raised his gaze to the other man's. "Are we clear?"

"Crystal." The man in the wingback chair smiled.

"Yes, sir," Underwood said and fled the room.

Chapter Ten

Emily stood beneath the hot spray of the shower and let the water beat down on her. She was so exhausted she felt as if her bones were melting. Her mind reeled with everything that had occurred in the last hours. She couldn't believe she was on the run for her life. That the people she'd spent the last three years working for were trying to kill her. That those same people were responsible for unspeakable acts of torture—and murder. That a man she was insanely attracted to was some kind of secret agent for some obscure government agency she'd never heard of.

Shutting off the squeaky old faucets, she stepped out of the shower and quickly dried herself. Her panties and bra were neatly draped over the shower rod, freshly washed. A white terry-cloth robe hung on a hook at the back of the door. Trying not to think of how she was going to feel facing Zack in nothing more than a robe, she slipped it on and knotted the belt at her waist.

"You're just tired, Monroe," she muttered as she wrapped her hair in a towel.

Not giving herself time to think about it, she swung open the door. The sight of Zack standing at the window without a shirt stopped her cold. Emily had seen plenty of male chests in her time. More often than not, she wasn't the least bit affected one way or another. But Zack Devlin's chest was a work of art. A masterpiece sculpted by an artist with an eye for sensual male beauty.

She felt his gaze on her as she moved to the table, but for the life of her she couldn't look at him. She didn't trust her expression not to give her away. Her cheeks were burning with a blush she couldn't seem to control. She couldn't stop thinking about what it had been like to kiss him….

"We need to talk," he said.

His words brought her out of her erotic reverie, and Emily glanced his way. He was looking at her as if she were a puzzle far beyond his capabilities. She could feel the zing of her pulse, her heart thumping against her ribs.

Tying the robe more tightly about her body, she sank onto the bed. For the first time it registered that there was only one bed in the room. That they were exhausted and badly in need of sleep if they were going to keep going. That she was suddenly filled with a strange sense of anticipation….

"I want you to tell me exactly why you became suspicious of Lockdown, Inc.," he said. "Only, I need details, dates and names this time."

"We've already been over this."

"We're missing something. Figuring out what that is is the only way we're going to get through this." Zack crossed to her and sat down on the bed. "I need to know everything, even if you think it may not be important."

He wasn't touching her, but Emily could feel the heat from his body, her nerves tingling in response. Steeling herself against feelings she didn't want to have, she folded her hands and looked down at them. "As a corrections officer, you get to know the inmates," she said. "Seeing them every day, you know which ones are trouble and which ones just want to do their time in peace. Even though we're trained never to get involved in any way with the inmates, the corrections officers are human beings. We talk to them. We get to like some of them."

She raised her gaze to Zack's, wondering if he could understand, if he had ever seen the corrections officers as anything but agents of humiliation and cruelty. "I was assigned to Big Jimmie Jack's cell block. In the three months I was there, I got to know him. I liked him, Zack. Even though he was a criminal, a lifer, he had lots of redeeming qualities I couldn't help but respond to. He had a good sense of humor. He was polite and liked to read Keats. He was a talented artist and painted several oil paintings a month. He was one of the ones who just wanted to do his time in peace. Over the months we developed a mutual respect for each other." Remembering, she pursed her lips. "Then one day he just disappeared. This big, burly, healthy guy. None of the other officers knew what had happened to him. I checked the infirmary report, but he wasn't listed."

"That was when you began investigating," Zack said.

She nodded. "It was then that I remembered one other inmate disappearing. Jinx Ramirez was different than Jimmie. He was always mouthing off. He assaulted one of the corrections officers and spent time in the Special Housing unit. I was assigned to him for a while, but I never liked him and I never trusted him. Before my assignment was up, he, too, disappeared. I didn't think too much about it, assuming he had been transferred. To be perfectly honest, I was relieved to be rid of him. But after Big Jimmie Jack disappeared, I started looking around. I found out Jinx Ramirez had also been sent to the infirmary. Like Big Jimmie Jack, Jinx didn't appear on the report and he never came out. At that point I remembered another incident a few months earlier involving an inmate who seemed healthy before going into the infirmary. When he came out, he was covered with lesions. He went into respiratory distress and died in his cell a few days later. At that point I started getting suspicious."

"Who did you talk to?"

"The other corrections officers at first. When they couldn't help, I went to my immediate supervisor, Sergeant Gaines."

"Jackson Gaines?"

She looked at him, surprised that he knew the name of her superior. "You know him?"

"Enough to know he's a ruthless son of a bitch."

"What makes you say that?"

Zack's jaw flexed. "I've read his profile, Emily."

"What profile?"

"The one MIDNIGHT put together before I went into that hellhole—and warned me that Gaines was in this up to his sergeant stripes."

"How is he involved?"

Zack scrubbed a hand over his unshaven jaw. "Several years ago Gaines was the warden in a prison outside Mexico City. We believe an organization based in Paris was manufacturing biological agents, shipping them to the prison for testing. Fifty-three inmates disappeared while Gaines was warden. We could never prove any of it."

"My God." For the first time the breadth of what was happening at the Bitterroot facility struck her. Nausea rose and she pressed her hand to her stomach. "We can't let this go on. We have to stop them."

"How well do you know Marcus Underwood?"

Absently she rubbed the bullet wound beneath the sleeve of her robe. "I've know him for three years. I can't reconcile myself to his being responsible for something so heinous."

"What about Warden Carpenter?"

She shook her head. "No way."

"Why?"

"Because I've known him since I was a teenager. My father worked for him. They were friends." *He was there for me after my father was killed*, a protective little voice chimed in.

"That makes him innocent?"

"I know him, Zack. Carpenter is a decent man. I can't imagine him being involved in something like…murder."

"Someone is."

"Not Carpenter."

Zack's expression told her he didn't share her view.

"What do we do next?" she asked.

He grimaced, looking suddenly as if the weight of the world had been lowered onto his broad shoulders. "Normally I would be able to call my contact at MIDNIGHT. They'd send someone to pick us up. Pick you up."

"But you can't because you're not sure who to trust," she said.

He nodded. "I need to figure out who at MIDNIGHT compromised this mission."

"Are you absolutely certain someone did? Maybe your identity was discovered some other way."

"The agency is extremely careful, Emily. They know an agent's cover can mean the difference between life and death."

A powerful chill swept through her as she realized what they were up against. "Do you have any enemies within the agency?"

He shook his head. "None that I know of."

"How many people knew about your mission?"

"Only a handful. My boss, Avery Shaw. My contact, a senior operative by the name of Tatum Massey. The two agents sent in with me. One or two administrative people." His gaze collided with hers. "All of these people are screened and hold high-security clearances."

"Why would someone betray you knowing you could be killed?"

He seemed to consider that a moment. "Money is the logical motivation. The RZ-902 operation is big and the financial stake is astronomical."

"How are you going to find them?"

"The same way you catch any rat," he said. "You set a trap."

Emily didn't like the sound of that. Traps required bait. She didn't want to think about what he might use as bait. Or what it might end up costing both of them. "What kind of trap do you have in mind?"

"I get to a phone. Call my regular contact. Set up a meet. If I get an ambush, I'll have found the rat."

"What if the rat kills you first?" Not liking the way the words felt on her tongue, she rose from the bed and began to pace the room.

"That's a chance I'll have to take."

She shook her head. "Too dangerous. We have to find another way."

"There is no 'we,' Emily. I've already told you too much. It ends here."

"It's my life you're talking about, Devlin. My conscience. My career. Everything I've ever worked for."

"We're not talking about your life. We're talking about your death." Something dark and frightening flashed in his eyes. "I want no part of that. Do you understand?"

"I'm not going to sit around and do nothing while these people continue to torture and maim and murder. I'm involved, damn it."

"What do you suggest?"

"I don't know!" To her horror, her voice cracked on the last word. She knew it was the fatigue tearing down her defenses; she was so exhausted she couldn't think straight.

Because she didn't want Zack to see just how close she was to a meltdown, she turned and started for the bathroom. She was almost there when a strong hand landed on her shoulder and spun her around.

"I don't want anything to happen to you, Emily. Before I can keep you safe, I need your cooperation."

She could feel the tears building and fought them valiantly. Emily didn't cry often. She'd always seen tears as a sign of weakness. But she was tired and scared and in so far over her head she didn't know what to do next. She didn't know who to trust.

"I can't stand the thought of those men dying because I didn't do anything to stop it," she said.

"This is not your fault."

"I'm part of Lockdown, Inc. I've worked at the Bitterroot facility for three years."

"You had no way of knowing what they were doing."

She wanted desperately to believe him, but in

some small, unreasonable part of her mind she'd already taken responsibility. Blinking back tears, she met his gaze levelly. "I'm going to be involved whether you like it or not."

"You don't know the extent of this. Damn it, you don't know what you're getting into."

"I know enough. I will not stand aside and let it happen. I can't do that any more than you can. I need to do this," she whispered. "Please. Let me help you stop this."

"Why, for God's sake?" he shouted.

"Because I need to be able to live with myself!"

He stared hard at her for a long, uncomfortable moment. The only sound came from the wind tearing around the window, the occasional ping of heat from the woodstove.

"Emily…"

In the next instant, the dynamics of the situation capitulated. Zack's expression changed from strained to slightly baffled. Intensity burned in his eyes as his gaze swept down her face and stopped on her mouth. Suddenly she was keenly aware of his proximity. That he was tall and muscular and devastatingly male. That her senses were humming with a tension that had nothing to do with Lockdown, Inc. and everything to do with the man standing so close she could hear the hiss of his breath.

She stared at him, wanting to deny what she knew would happen next. Something that was every bit as dangerous to her as the men chasing them but in a very different way. Her intellect told her to turn and

walk away. It reminded her that she should be concentrating on the mystery and not this man who
seemed to put her under a spell every time he touched
her.

But Emily's heart betrayed her intellect. When he
leaned close and set his mouth against hers, all
thought of pulling away and doing the right thing
evaporated as the pleasure sank in and went all the
way through her.

Need pulsed when his arms went around her.
Heat surged when he pulled her against him. His
body was like hot steel against hers. She could feel
the hard ridge of his arousal against her cleft, sliding and seeking…her. Desire flashed, then spread
like wildfire. She could feel it leaping though her
body like flames, burning her, frightening her with
its unleashed power.

Emily had had two serious relationships in her
life. But nothing she'd ever experienced had prepared her for the way this man kissed her. Or for the
way her body responded.

Her arms went around his neck. As if by its own
accord, her body shifted against his shaft.

An instant later he shoved her to arm's length.
The action startled her, breaking the spell of her
desire-induced haze. His hands were tight around
her arms as he stared down at her, his pupils so dilated they looked black.

"What the hell do you think you're doing?" he
said sharply.

She blinked, stunned as much by the unreasonable question as by his angry tone. "I could ask you the same thing," she replied, equally sharply.

Releasing her abruptly, he stumbled back, staring at her as if he'd just realized she was a danger to him. "I'm going to take a shower," he said.

"Devlin—"

"Get some sleep." Turning away from her, he crossed to the bathroom, stepped inside and slammed the door behind him.

Chapter Eleven

Zack didn't bother with the hot water. Not that the cold water was helping much. He'd been standing beneath the spray for going on ten minutes and his erection was showing no signs of abating anytime soon.

So much for keeping a professional distance.

"You're a bloody idiot," he muttered as he rinsed the soap from his face.

Cursing, he switched off the water and yanked a towel off the rack. When was he going to learn that women and undercover work were a deadly mix? Hadn't he learned his lesson with Alisa?

The thought of the female agent who'd lost her life because of him twisted his gut into an all too familiar knot. Two years ago he and Alisa Hayes had partnered to work on breaking up a terrorist camp in the west Texas desert. It had been a tough assignment. Zack and Alisa had approached the group passing as illegal-weapons brokers and had infiltrated the group. But instead of concentrating solely on the mission, Alisa had ended up in his tent one night and Zack hadn't sent her away.

After that encounter, Zack had lost all objectivity. He'd lost his concentration. His focus. By the time he realized he'd screwed up, it was too late. Alisa was dead and Avery Shaw had a bullet in his spine. Was Zack going to make the same mistake all over again with Emily?

Zack flung open the door. He couldn't believe he was getting himself into the same mess. Two people he'd cared deeply for had paid a very steep price because he hadn't had the discipline to keep his hands off—

The sight of Emily curled on the bed, fast asleep, stopped him cold. She was lying on her side with her arms crossed, her face relaxed. Her lashes were like black velvet against her pale complexion. Her full lips were partially open and looked incredibly inviting, reminding him of what it had been like to kiss her. The robe she was wearing had ridden up slightly, and he could see the velvet flesh of her thighs. For a full minute he stood there captivated, watching her sleep.

Zack knew better than to take those few treacherous steps to the bed. If he got any closer, he would touch her. And this time he wouldn't stop with just touching her. Considering the way she'd responded just a few minutes earlier, he wasn't certain she would either. A disaster waiting to happen.

So how are you going to keep her safe when you've got your hands all over her? The same way you kept Alisa safe?

Ignoring the hot rush of blood to his groin, Zack crossed to her. Standing at the edge of the bed, he gazed down at her. She was long legs and lush flesh rolled into a tempting-as-hell package. He could smell the shampoo and soap she'd used in her recent shower. He'd seen her panties and bra hanging neatly in the bathroom and knew she wasn't wearing a thing beneath that robe....

"Don't even go there," he muttered, bending to her.

She groaned and shifted restlessly when he pulled the down comforter up and over her. "Zack?"

"Go to sleep," he whispered.

But Zack knew that was the one thing that would not come to him right now.

EMILY WOKE WITH A START and she sat up. Bright sunlight spilled in through a single draped window. The air smelled slightly of wood smoke. Briefly she was disoriented, not remembering where she was. Then she remembered Zack Devlin. The situation at Lockdown, Inc. Going into Signal Research and Development. The chase through the night. And that hot, hot kiss they'd shared.

She knew without even glancing around that Zack was gone. He was the kind of man whose presence she could feel. Even with her eyes closed she would know if he was in the room. She tried to deny the stab of disappointment, to deny that she'd been looking forward to seeing him.

Tossing off the comforter, she padded to the bathroom, then she switched on the television. The four-cup coffeemaker was on and half-full, so she poured herself a cup. A news story on the TV grabbed her attention as she took her first sip.

"There was an escape last night from the Bitter-root maximum-security prison near Salmon." The pretty blond reporter's eyes sparkled with excitement as she read the news report. "Irish terrorist Zack McKinnon, who is serving a life sentence on multiple counts of murder, escaped last night with the help of a female corrections officer. The jailbreak left two inmates dead and launched the largest manhunt this peaceful, rural area has ever seen. The manhunt is continuing this morning."

"What?" Emily nearly choked on her coffee. Her gut tightened when both her and Zack's photos flashed on the screen.

The reporter continued. "Channel 53 was on the scene first thing this morning and got the following statement from prison administrator Marcus Underwood."

Underwood stepped up to the mike. "At approximately three o'clock this morning, convicted Irish terrorist Zack McKinnon murdered two fellow inmates and, with the help of a female corrections officer, escaped. Lockdown, Inc. is using every resource available, including local law enforcement and our own SORT team, to apprehend this convicted killer and his accomplice."

A second stark black-and-white photo flashed on the screen. Emily's stomach began to churn. It was the security-camera photo taken in the prison locker room the moment Zack had kissed her. Her arms were around his neck, their bodies locked in a tight embrace.

"Oh, no," Emily whispered.

The reporter continued. "Mr. Underwood, how do you explain this photo from the prison security cameras?"

Underwood frowned. "We feel that this female officer is confused and has inadvertently placed herself in grave danger. We appeal to her to turn herself over to authorities."

"What can you tell us about McKinnon?" the reporter asked.

"He is responsible for the deaths of many people in Belfast, Ireland, as well as a triple homicide in Chicago three years ago. He is a violent sociopath, a con and a highly persuasive liar capable of elaborate schemes."

"Is it true that this female corrections officer helped him escape?"

"We believe he convinced her that he is innocent. We believe she may be trying to help him when in reality she has put herself and our community at great risk. We appeal to both Ms. Monroe and McKinnon to turn themselves in."

"What should someone do if they see them?" the reporter asked.

"Above all else, do not approach them. Both individuals are armed and should be considered extremely dangerous. Call Lockdown, Inc. or local law enforcement immediately."

Two phone numbers flashed on the screen, but Emily barely heard the reporter recite them. Underwood's words about Zack rang in her ears as loudly as the report of a gun. *He is a violent sociopath, a con and a highly persuasive liar capable of elaborate schemes.*

Doubt once again rose inside her. Had Zack manipulated her? Had he lied to her to gain her trust? Was she making the same mistakes her father had made all those years ago?

Like father, like daughter....

She'd heard those words a thousand times as a teenager. Even though her father's mistakes had been too complex for her to fully comprehend then, she'd hated him for humiliating her and her mother.

As an adult, Emily understood all too well what he'd done. Adam Monroe had sold his soul for a moment of physical pleasure with a female inmate. He'd traded his uniform, his self-respect and his dignity for sex.

And now she was making the same mistake.

"What have I done?" she whispered.

Rising, she darted to the bathroom, ripped off the robe and stepped into her clean underclothes. Yanking her uniform off the hook behind the door, she quickly dressed. Back in the room, she began to lace her boots. She wasn't going to throw her life away because she was attracted to a smooth-talking con. She sure as hell wasn't going to make the same mistake her father had made. She was going to go back to the prison and straighten things out.

She was striding to the door, yanking on her coat as she went, when it swung open. Zack stepped into the room. She froze as he took her measure. The boots. Her coat.

"Going somewhere?" he asked.

"I'm going back to the prison to get things straightened out."

His gaze bore into her. "Why the change of heart?"

"Because I know what you are."

"And what is that?"

"You're a con, a liar and a murderer."

His gaze flicked to the television and then back to her. "Don't believe what you hear on television."

"Why wouldn't I?" Logic told her he was right; she'd seen the evidence they'd unearthed back at the laboratory. But it was confusion and emotion driving her, a fire driven by fear because her feelings for Zack had grown to dangerous proportions.

"They'll kill you if you go back," he said evenly.

"I'll take my chances. At least with Lockdown I know where I stand." She tried to brush past him, but he caught her arm.

Emily was ready for him. Swinging around, she shoved hard against his shoulder, hoping to propel herself back and through the door. But Zack was faster and countered her move by tightening his grip and pulling her toward him. Momentarily off balance, Emily stumbled. The next thing she knew, her body was flush against his. His eyes were dark with anger as they searched her face.

"I can't let you walk out that door," he said.

"Did you lie to me, Zack? Use me?"

"If I was interested in using you, I would have had you in my bed by now."

She drew back to slap him, but he caught her wrist before her palm made contact with his face.

"I don't know what you think you know, but I've never lied to you," he said.

"I saw a news report, Zack. I know about your past. I know you're a murderer. A terrorist."

His lips pulled back in a sneer. "That's a lie."

"The local police are involved. I'm in serious trouble. They think I helped you escape." Emily tried to twist away, but he tightened his grip and shook her gently.

"Listen to me," he said. "I set up a meeting with my contact from MIDNIGHT. I have to be at the rendezvous point in half an hour."

"MIDNIGHT doesn't exist! It's all a big lie."

"Where is this coming from?" he asked.

"Lying is what you do, isn't it, Zack? You lie to win someone's trust? How do you do it? Do you lie to yourself, too? Is that how you live with yourself?"

"You don't believe that."

There was a part of her that desperately wanted to believe Zack. She needed to know she wasn't like her father. But what about the news report?

"Give me a chance to prove to you I'm not lying," he said.

Staring into his dark eyes, she could feel her

emotions spiralling. How could she feel this way about a man who may have murdered innocent people?

"Let go of me," she said.

"Not a chance," he said and lowered his mouth to hers.

ZACK KNEW BETTER THAN TO fight fire with fire. He knew he was only going to get burned. But he couldn't stand the way she was looking at him. As if he were the lowest form of life on the planet. As if he were a killer and a liar and she didn't believe a word he said.

He wasn't quite sure when he'd started to care what she thought of him. But he did. Too much, if he wanted to be honest about it. Not because he needed her help. But because he couldn't bear the thought of her believing he was a killer.

For the span of several seconds she fought him. She set her hands against his chest and pushed. But then her body went soft and slack against his. A sigh whispered across his cheek. The protest she was in the process of uttering came out as a moan. Then she was kissing him back and he forgot all about the mission, about crossing lines, about being a professional and doing the right thing.

Touching her had unleashed something inside him. Made him just a little bit insane. Insane to kiss her. To touch her. To be inside her.

Suddenly he realized they were standing at the front door, with cold air pouring in. Never taking his mouth from hers, he pushed her into the room, closed the door and locked it. Then they were on the bed and he was unbuttoning her shirt. Need like he'd never known before churned inside him.

Her shirt fell open. Zack's gaze swept over her breasts, and he was awed by the sheer perfection of her. That she would share this with him moved him. He could feel his emotions intensifying, making him feel things he did not want to feel. This was not the time for him to go off the deep end.

But then, he'd never had the best of timing when it came to women.

She quivered when he touched her breast.

Uncharacteristically uncertain, he ran his hands over her thin cotton bra with a feather touch. "Let me touch you."

He didn't wait for her permission and with the flick of his wrist unsnapped the front closure of her bra. The scrap of material fell open. Her nipples were large and erect, her belly taut and flat. When he looked into her eyes, he didn't see a corrections officer but a woman he very much wanted to make love to.

"Emily…"

He kissed her hard on the mouth, then pulled back, shaken and awed. Her eyes shimmered. He saw uncertainty in their depths and put his hands on either side of her face, forcing her gaze to his. "I need for you to trust me," he whispered.

"I'm afraid."

"Of me?"

"Of what I feel for you. It's messing with my head."

His need for her was making it increasingly difficult for him to concentrate. He wanted her trust, but he'd reached a point where he could no longer keep himself from touching her.

"Me, too," he said softly. "Trust your heart."

The kiss was electric and he felt it all the way to his toes. He could feel his control slipping away, leaving him raw and aching with desire for this beautiful woman in front of him. He heard his name on her lips. Felt her arms going around him—

Pounding at the door sent Zack scrambling off the bed. Out of the corner of his eye he saw Emily sitting, clutching her shirt to her breasts, her eyes wide and frightened. Then Zack's training kicked in. He darted for the disguise he'd used the night before. Standing in front of the mirror, he went to work.

A second knock sounded, harder and more impatient. "This is the Lemhi County Sheriff's Department. Open the door, we're checking all the rooms."

Though his heart was pounding, Zack's hands were steady as he used the adhesive to secure the tiny mustache to his upper lip. The scar came next. No time to finesse. His gaze met Emily's in the mirror and he whispered, "Get dressed. Pack what you can. Hide in the shower, close the curtain, take your bag with you."

She was already off the bed and heading toward the bathroom. He watched the light in the bathroom go out. Saw the door close halfway. Heard the shower curtain hiss as she yanked it closed.

Praying the police didn't force their way in and search the room, Zack crossed to the door, slipped into his antiquarian persona and opened the door.

Chapter Twelve

Emily crouched in the bathtub, expecting that at any moment the bathroom door would burst open, the shower curtain yanked aside and strong hands would reach in to haul her off to jail for aiding and abetting an escaped convict.

Fighting panic, she closed her eyes and prayed Zack was a good enough actor to convince the police he was a traveling salesman and that he was alone in the room.

A full minute passed before she calmed down enough to listen to what was going on. The conversation was muffled because the bathroom door was partially closed. But the voices were loud enough for her to make out most of what was being said.

"You're here alone?" asked an authoritative male voice.

"I'm quite alone. In fact, I was going to be checking out in a few minutes. Is everything all right?"

It took Emily a moment to recognize Zack's voice. The Irish brogue had been replaced by a Boston inflection.

"There's an escaped convict in the vicinity," the male voice said. "We're canvassing the area. Checking with the ranchers and motel owners and alerting the park rangers."

"Is this person dangerous?" Zack asked.

"Armed and extremely dangerous. He's traveling with a woman. She's a corrections officer we believe is helping him. If you see either of them, use your cell phone to call 911."

"Of course. I hope you catch them."

"So do we."

The door slammed. Emily nearly fainted with relief. She was in the process of stepping out of the shower when Zack walked in. Had the situation not been so potentially threatening, she might have laughed at the sight of him. He looked like a meek bookworm, with his small mustache, spectacles, pinched expression and hunched shoulders. She didn't know when he'd done it, but he'd even added colored contact lenses. The transformation was truly amazing.

"That was damn close," he said, the old Zack returning.

"What do we do now?" she asked.

"We need transportation." He glanced at the alarm clock next to the bed. "I can't miss that meeting I set up with my contact from MIDNIGHT."

"How do we get a vehicle?"

"Since we can't buy one, we're going to have to borrow one."

She didn't like the way he'd used the word *bor-*

row. It sounded too much like *steal* and, with the police hot on their trail, the fastest way to get caught.

"This place is crawling with cops," she said. "How on earth are we going to steal a car?"

"There's a service station down the road. I discovered it when I left to use the phone earlier this morning. The service station is closed on Sunday, but they have several cars sitting in the lot, waiting to be serviced."

"Terrific. We get a car that's kaput."

He grinned. "We get a car no one will miss until tomorrow."

Emily was about to nix the idea when he leaned forward and kissed her. The combination of adrenaline and lust was heady, and she kissed him back. She knew it was risky, reacting to him like this when they were a hairbreadth away from getting caught—or worse. But it was as if he'd put her under some kind of spell. A spell that was going to at the very least ruin her career. At the very worst get her killed.

His eyes clashed with hers when he pulled back. "Hold that thought," he said. "I'll meet you in the rear lot in five minutes."

ZACK CHOSE the four-wheel-drive Jeep with tires the size of boulders and keys in the ignition, and five minutes later he and Emily were on the main road heading north toward the rendezvous point he'd set up with his contact from MIDNIGHT.

The last thing Zack had wanted to do was take Emily with him. There was a good possibility they were walking into an ambush. He'd considered dropping her off at the local sheriff's office, but he knew she would be no safer in the hands of law enforcement. The Lockdown people had fabricated a story and put out a press release; the police now believed she was an accomplice to murder. There was no safe haven to stash her, so he'd had no choice but to bring her along. He only hoped his decision wouldn't cost her her life.

Sitting quietly in the passenger seat, Emily was distant, staring out the window as if the snowy landscape beyond held the answers she so desperately needed. Zack wished he could say something to reassure her, but he was fresh out of solutions.

It was the shadows in her eyes that bothered him most.

"What's on your mind?" he asked when the silence grew oppressive.

"I don't see how we're going to win this." She gave him a long, assessing look. "The police think you're a killer. They think I'm your accomplice."

"We'll get through this." He reached over and set his hand over hers. "I want you to know, if it's the last thing I do, I'm going to make sure your name is cleared."

Lowering her head, she sighed. "I don't know who I am anymore, Zack."

"You're a decent human being who's risking her life to do the right thing."

She raised her head, her gaze searching his. "Or maybe I'm here because…" Another sigh shuddered out of her. "Because every time you look at me, every time you touch me, I forget about doing the right thing." She grabbed the breast pocket of her coat where the Lockdown logo was silk-screened into the fabric. "This logo, this uniform, used to mean something to me. It used to mean everything to me. I've thrown it all away—"

"Emily, we're in a high-adrenaline situation. We've been under an incredible amount of stress for over thirty-six hours—"

"This isn't about adrenaline or stress or even the amount of time we've spent together."

"No, but those things can complicate an already complicated situation. Especially when the chemistry between two people is right."

"Or maybe history is repeating itself."

"What are you talking about?"

She surprised him by laughing, but it was a bitter sound. A sound he didn't like coming from her. "Maybe I really am like my father."

He didn't know anything about her father. But Zack saw clearly the rise of emotion in her face. He saw it in the way her hands had begun to shake. He heard it in the tremor in her voice. And he knew that whatever she was about to tell him was deeply painful for her.

"What does this have to do with your father?" he asked.

"You mean you don't know about the infamous Adam Monroe?"

Zack waited, sensing she needed to talk, knowing he was going to have to push to get her to open up. He glanced in the rearview mirror, watching for flashing lights or a car following too closely or for too long. Snowflakes had begun to fall from the gray sky, but he didn't think it was going to storm.

He waited for her to speak. When she didn't, he said softly, "Talk to me, Emily. Tell me what happened to your father."

"He was a corrections officer for the state of Idaho," she began. "He worked his way up through the ranks all the way to lieutenant. He was good at what he did. He was professional and respected. When I was fifteen, he was transferred to the Balpost Correctional Facility for women. There had been some problems at the prison and they sent my father there to implement some new policies and procedures and straighten things out." She looked down at her hands and sighed. "He was there for only six months when the problems began. I was too young to fully understand what was going on. But I heard the phone calls. I heard arguments between him and my mother. I saw the articles in the local paper, the reports on the local news. I heard the whispers behind my back when I was at school."

"What happened?"

"My father…became involved with a female inmate."

Shock and compassion rippled through him. And finally he understood why she'd been so very reluctant to believe him, to trust him. "I'm sorry."

"I was too young to understand all the implications. Both of my parents tried to shield me from most of it. But I knew he'd done something…reprehensible."

"Something like that is tough for a fifteen-year-old girl to grasp."

"It was a terrible time for my family," she said. "There was a lot of arguing. Phone calls in the middle of the night. Visits from the police. My mother was furious. She said he shamed us. He shamed his profession."

"How did it happen? I mean, were there mitigating circumstances? A question of this female inmate's guilt? What?"

"I don't know. He never told us."

"You mean he didn't defend himself? Wasn't there some kind of formal hearing or charges filed against him? Did he lose his job?"

"He didn't live long enough to tell us what had happened."

"I'm sorry." Zack looked away from the road to stare at her, his mind reeling, his heart hurting for the fifteen-year-old girl she'd been. "How did it happen?"

"He committed suicide."

"Aw, man. Emily…"

"It was a long time ago." She lifted one shoulder, let it fall. "It was tough. But I worked through it. I'm okay now."

He grimaced, knowing she was not. "What happened to the female inmate?"

"I don't know."

"Who was she?"

"Her name was Shanna James. I've seen photographs, and she was very beautiful and very young. Just ten years older than I was at the time." She smiled, but it was humorless, brittle. "She'd been in prison for two years when they met. She had been convicted of murdering her husband."

"Nice."

"From what I was able to piece together, she targeted my father. Used every enticement in the book, including her body." She closed her eyes, as if the pain of what she was about to say was too much to bear. "He sacrificed everything to be with her. His career. His family. His very life. I hate to say it, but I think he was actually in love with her."

Zack didn't know what to say, so he let her talk.

"My parents had been having problems. Once my father's indiscretion was made public, my mother filed for divorce. He moved out. Two weeks later he was dead."

"That must have been incredibly painful for you."

"All I wanted was for my parents to get back together. I hated the woman who took that away from me. I hated him for being weak and letting it happen." She pressed the heels of her hands to her eyes, then let her hands fall to her lap. "And then he was dead and I had no one left to be angry with."

"This is why you've been so resistant to believing me."

"It's why I've been cautious."

He looked at her, wishing he wasn't driving so

he could reach out and touch her and somehow make her believe he was telling the truth. "Your father was human, Emily. Sometimes human beings make mistakes."

"I won't make the same mistakes he did."

Her words rang hollowly inside the cab of the Jeep, and Zack felt them like a punch to the solar plexus. They were only a few minutes from the rendezvous point he'd set up at a scenic overlook, but all he could think about was Emily and what she'd been through, what he was putting her through now.

I won't make the same mistakes he did.

The sign for the scenic overlook flashed by. Zack slowed the Jeep, spotted the exit just ahead. Next to him Emily had turned her attention back to the window, shutting him out as effectively as the glass shut out the cold. He knew it was stupid at a time when he needed to be concentrating on his upcoming meeting, but he wanted her trust so badly he could taste it.

Zack drove past the exit.

"You just missed it," Emily said.

"I'm going to park a few hundred yards down."

"Are you anticipating problems?"

"That appears to be the theme of this mission." Spotting a gravel shoulder, Zack slowed the Jeep and pulled over. Unfastening his safety belt, he turned to Emily. "Get in the driver's seat," he said.

Her eyes widened. "What?"

"I'm going to leave the keys in the ignition," he said. "If anything happens, I want you to drive to the next county and go directly to the sheriff's office. Tell them everything."

"Zack, in case you've missed a few details in the last day or so, I'm a fugitive just like you."

"The mole will kill you on sight, no questions asked. So will Underwood and his goons at Lockdown, Inc. The police are your only recourse if we get ambushed."

"The police could be part of this."

"That's why I'm telling you to drive to the next county. Not every cop in this state is on the take. Now, damn it, slide over to the driver's seat."

She climbed over the console. When she'd settled behind the wheel, he reached for the handle and stepped out of the Jeep.

"Zack?"

His gaze collided with hers, and he felt the impact like a speeding truck. She looked beautiful and frightened, and it took every ounce of willpower he possessed not to lean into the Jeep and crush his mouth to hers.

"Be careful," she said.

Giving her what he hoped was a reassuring smile, he slammed the door and started toward the overlook a hundred yards away.

EMILY SAT BEHIND THE WHEEL, staring at the keys dangling from the ignition. If she wanted to leave, all she had to do was reach down, start the engine and she'd be home free.

Do it! Save yourself. Your reputation.

She's just like her old man....

Emily put her fingers on the keys, but she didn't start the engine. She couldn't leave now. Not only because she knew her employers at Lockdown, Inc. were responsible for countless crimes but because at some point—and despite her resolve not to—she had come to care for Zack. There was no way she could leave him alone in such a perilous situation.

What kind of person did that make her? she wondered. Like her father? Was Emily making the same mistake he had all over again?

"Enough," she told herself.

She leaned back in the seat and looked around. In the last twenty minutes or so the sky had darkened and begun to spit snow. Because of slippery conditions remaining from the day before, the highway was all but deserted. Turning in the seat, she tried to spot Zack, but he'd already reached the overlook. She was about to turn back around when she noticed movement in the scrub brush thirty feet above the overlook.

Terror struck her like a bolt of lightning when she realized she was looking at a man with a rifle set up on a tripod. Not a hunter or a rancher but a man wearing a dark trench coat, and he was seconds away from killing Zack.

Without considering her own safety, she threw open the door and started toward the overlook at a dead run. She wanted to call out to Zack, to warn him that he'd walked into an ambush, but she feared the sniper would fire prematurely. All she could do was run as fast as she could and hope she got there in time.

Her boots pounded against icy asphalt as she rounded the curve in the road. She spotted Zack standing at the rail, looking out over a magnificent snow-covered valley below. Though he stood ready, as if anticipating trouble, his back was to the rise. There was no way he could see the sniper.

Torn between warning him and alerting the sniper that he'd been seen, Emily stood motionless for the span of two heartbeats. Then she screamed, "Gun! Zack! Behind you!"

He spun. Myriad emotions scrolled across his face. Pleasure at seeing her. Fear for her safety. The realization that he'd made a fatal mistake.

The gunshot split the air like a crack of thunder. As if in slow motion, Zack jolted. For a moment he looked stunned. Then his hands clutched his abdomen. Emily saw blood coming between his fingers. And then he crumpled to the ground.

"No!" Forgetting her own safety, she streaked toward him.

As she covered the snowy ground, she saw the gunman out of the corner of her eye. The black flash of the barrel as he lined up for another shot. He was on a rise less than thirty feet away from where Zack had fallen. The logical side of her brain told her she was next. But it was her heart, not logic, that sent her barreling toward Zack.

Dear God, he couldn't be dead.

She was so intent on reaching him that she didn't hear the second shot.

Chapter Thirteen

Zack had gotten kicked by a horse when he was twelve years old. One moment he'd been standing there watching Katie Murdoch throw on the saddle and tighten the cinch. The next he'd had a steel shoe planted in the general vicinity of his solar plexus with a thousand pounds of thrust behind it.

Getting shot wasn't much different, he thought as he lay on the ground and tried to get oxygen into his lungs. He could feel shock stealing his thoughts. Then his training kicked in. He rolled once and staggered to his feet. He knew it wouldn't be long before the sniper fired again. He had to find cover.

Then he saw Emily running toward him and his only thought was that the damn crazy woman was going to get herself shot.

Just like Alisa.

"Emily, no!" Clutching his side where the bullet had struck him, Zack leaped into a run toward her. "Go back to the Jeep!"

She stopped and stood there, hesitating. He imagined her lovely face in the crosshairs of a sniper scope and he panicked. "Go back!"

She turned as if in slow motion. Zack poured on the speed and followed. Somewhere in the distance a bullet ricocheted off rock. Running at full speed, Zack placed himself between Emily and the sniper. "Get in the Jeep!" he shouted.

He was just ten feet away from her when they reached the Jeep. She ran to the passenger side, flung open the door and dived onto the seat. Zack yanked open the driver's-side door, twisted the key. The Jeep shot forward before he'd even closed his door, its wheels slinging snow and slush and gravel high into the air.

For several seconds the only sound came from the roar of the engine and the ragged hiss of their labored breathing. Jamming the gears with a tad too much force, Zack pushed the vehicle to a dangerous speed. He didn't know if it was the pain in his abdomen or the remnants of fear, but he was suddenly furious with Emily.

"What the bloody hell do you think you were doing?" he demanded.

"I saw the sniper," she said between breaths. "Before the gunshot. I was trying to warn you."

"You just about got yourself killed, damn it!"

"Zack, calm down."

"Like *hell!*"

"Zack, please...you've been shot."

"You think I don't know that?" He rapped his

hand hard against the steering wheel. "Damn it, Emily. You scared the hell out of me!"

"Look, there was no way I could sit there and do nothing while that sniper picked you off."

He looked away from the road to glare at her, felt another wave of terror envelop him. He would never be able to live with himself if anything happened to her. Why in the name of God had he dragged her into this? What was he supposed to do now?

"Was that the mole?" she asked after a moment.

"I didn't get a good look at him." But he knew he'd just had a close encounter with the man who'd betrayed him. There was only a handful of people who'd known he would be there. His contact at MIDNIGHT. Avery Shaw. An administrative clerk by the name of Watson. He wondered which one of them wanted him dead and why. Did it have something to do with Lockdown, Inc.?

"He almost killed you, Zack. What are we going to do?"

"We don't have a whole lot of options," he said, hating it because for the first time in his life he was flat out of ideas.

"Maybe we could go back to the bed-and-breakfast," she suggested.

"They've seen my face."

"They only saw you with the disguise."

He felt her eyes on him, and then she gasped. "Zack, you're gushing blood."

He looked down, saw blood pouring through his

coat and cursed between clenched teeth. Damn, it ticked him off when people shot at him.

"Swell." He shifted his gaze from the road to Emily to the rearview mirror. He could feel the warmth of blood on his shirt beneath his coat. He didn't think it was more than a flesh wound; he wouldn't be able to function if the bullet had penetrated his gut. Still, the damn thing hurt like a son of a bitch.

"We need to stop," she said.

"We've no place to stop," he said tightly.

"My dad used to own an old hunting cabin not far from here. He left it to me when he died."

"How far?"

"About fifteen miles south of Shoup. In the Salmon National Forest. There's a dirt road."

Zack figured it was the best they could hope for. He only hoped the police—or his pals from MID-NIGHT—hadn't done their research thoroughly. Because if they had, there was no doubt in his mind someone would be waiting when he and Emily arrived.

THE SNOW MADE THE NARROW mountain road a nightmare to maneuver. Even with the four-wheel drive, the Jeep got stuck twice along the way. But with some pushing and cursing and a little bit of luck, Zack finally pulled into the snow-covered driveway of the cabin and parked beneath a thick stand of ponderosa pines.

He'd been quiet for the last ten minutes of the

drive. At Emily's urging they'd stopped at a service station for first-aid supplies. Zack had forced her to wear the mustache and glasses. She wasn't sure what the clerk had thought, but she was relatively certain he hadn't recognized her face.

Emily slid from the Jeep into a foot of snow. Zack was already close to the cabin. She didn't like the way he was moving—hunched over as if he were in pain. She prayed the bullet wound wasn't serious because she knew he would refuse to go to the hospital.

The cabin was small. The front porch sagged a little more than she remembered. The tin roof was rusted through in places and in dire need of repair. Surprisingly most of the windows were still intact. On the porch she came up behind Zack as he tried the front door.

"Locked," he said. "Do you have a key?"

She shook her head. "We'll have to find another way to—"

Zack smashed his elbow through the small pane closest to the bolt lock. "You can bill me later," he said and opened the door.

The cabin smelled of ancient wood and dust motes. The floorboards creaked like old bones as they stepped inside. "This place have electricity?" he asked.

"No."

"Terrific."

"There's a fireplace. And there should be a kerosene lamp or two."

"Better than spending the night in the snow."

"Or in jail."

He turned to her and his expression softened. "Sorry I snapped at you earlier."

"It's okay. You're hurting."

"Yeah, and pain really ticks me off." He touched the side of her face with the backs of his fingers. "I'll build a fire. Why don't you see if you can round up those kerosene lamps you mentioned?"

She tilted her head slightly, pressing her cheek into his hand. She knew it was silly, but the small contact felt incredibly reassuring. "Deal," she said.

Ten minutes later Emily had located two kerosene lamps. The wick had rotted in one of them, so she set it aside and lit the single remaining lamp. Zack had managed to find some dry wood and was kneeling in front of a blazing fire. He'd shaken the dust from a Navajo-print rug and spread it on the floor.

"That ought to warm it up in here enough to keep us from freezing to death during the night," Zack said, sitting back on his heels.

Emily knelt beside him. "I need to see to that gunshot wound."

She could tell he wanted to argue, but he was smart enough to know he couldn't let a potentially serious injury go untreated. Neither of them had any idea when or if he would be able to seek medical help.

Grimacing, he motioned toward an Adirondack chair a few feet from the hearth. "That okay?"

"It'll do." Turning away from him, she dragged the

small end table to the chair and set the kerosene lamp on its dusty surface. Behind her she could hear Zack taking off his coat. She knew it was silly, but the thought of facing his bare chest made her mouth go dry. Gathering the first-aid supplies, she turned to him.

He was standing next to the chair watching her. She stood mesmerized as his hands moved down the front of his shirt, unfastening the buttons. Never taking his eyes from hers, he worked the shirt from his body. Light from the hearth flickered over bronzed skin and muscles that rippled when he moved. His chest was wide and covered with a thatch of black hair that tapered to the waistband of his trousers.

There were a thousand reasons why she shouldn't be attracted to this man, but she was. And that attraction was pulling at her, like some volatile chemical reaction that would invariably burn them both.

She set the tray on the table. "Sit down."

Wincing a little, Zack lowered himself into the chair and leaned back. For the first time Emily was able to get a good look at the gunshot wound. The bullet had opened the skin and caused a deep gash a couple of inches above his navel. There was some swelling and bruising, but the bullet hadn't entered his body. Relief poured through her when she realized it wasn't life threatening.

"I think this is a superficial wound," she said. "Like mine was."

"Doesn't feel superficial. Hurts like hell."

"It could have been a lot worse."

Her hands were shaking when she picked up the bottle of peroxide and a sterile gauze pad. Emily knew this was no time to be taken in by this man's charms—all one million of them. But the sight of Zack Devlin slouched in that chair was enough to make any woman long to be reckless.

"This is probably going to hurt a little," she said.

"It's probably going to hurt a lot."

She drizzled some peroxide over the wound, then began to clean it. Zack's quick intake of breath told her it hurt. She could feel his abdominal muscles tensing.

"How bad?" he asked, his voice strained.

"It's a deep graze. You could probably use a few stitches, but I think I can close it with a butterfly bandage."

"Do what you need to do to keep me operational. Don't worry about hurting me. I can handle it."

But when she glanced up, she saw sweat beginning to bead on his forehead. "I'm sorry," she said. "I know this is painful."

"It doesn't hurt nearly as much as knowing you're still having a hard time trusting me."

Her hand stilled. "I don't have the power to hurt you."

"That's where you're wrong," he said baldly.

Unable to meet his gaze, she stared at her hand, pale against the dark hair of his abdomen, surprised to see that it was shaking.

"You're afraid that if you admit there's something between us, you'll be drawing some kind of parallel between you and what your father did."

"The parallels are there," she said.

"The circumstances are different. You're a different person than he was, Emily."

She needed to finish bandaging the wound so she could put some distance between them, but her fingers kept fumbling the gauze.

"Look at me," he said gently.

"I just want to finish this," she said, staring at the wound.

Somehow she managed to press the bandage into place. But her hands were still visibly shaking. She knew Zack had noticed. She could feel his eyes on her. The heat rising from his body. She could feel her own body responding to all of those things.

"Why are you shaking?" Putting his fingers beneath her chin, he forced her gaze to his. And then she was staring into his dark eyes. She could feel the tremors moving through her body. Her breaths coming short and fast. She didn't know what was happening to her. All she knew was that no man had ever looked at her the way Zack Devlin did. No man had ever affected her the way he did. No man had ever made her want with such total and utter desperation.

"Trust yourself, Emily," he said darkly. "Trust your heart. Trust me."

She was standing over him, looking down. In a single smooth motion he reached up, set his hand behind her neck and pulled her mouth to his.

The pleasure was instant and intense. She didn't even realize her knees had buckled until they hit the floor with a quiet thud. In the next instant he was out of the chair, pushing her back onto the Navajo rug and coming down on top of her.

His kisses stole her breath. Her body flamed with need. She could feel dampness spreading between her legs, the desire that was a sharp ache verging on pain.

"Who are you, Zack Devlin?" she whispered.

"I'm the man who will never hurt you. The man who would give his own life to keep you safe. If you believe anything about me, believe that."

She believed him. There was no way he could look at her the way he did—kiss her the way he did—and not be telling the truth.

Pulling away slightly, he reached out and began unbuttoning her shirt. Neither of her previous two affairs had prepared her for the sensations coursing through her body or the emotions crowding into her heart. Deep inside she knew this was different. That this moment was profound. That it would change everything.

He worked the shirt from her shoulders. As he unfastened her bra, cold air whispered over her nipples as the scrap of cotton fell away.

"You're so beautiful," he said softly.

Leaning forward, he kissed her gently, his hands falling to her belt. She was breathing hard, shaking, anticipating the moment when he touched her….

Unable to keep herself from it, she ran her fingers over his hard-as-rock abdomen, careful to avoid the bandage. He shuddered and moaned low in his throat when she ran her fingers over his pebbled nipples. Then he was tugging her slacks down, and she kicked them off. Next came her panties. He quickly removed the rest of his clothes. Never taking his eyes from hers, he kissed her. A groan escaped her when he brushed his palms over her breasts. Then he was touching her belly, caressing her hips, then the tender flesh between her legs. Sensation swamped her when he slipped two fingers inside her and began to stroke her.

She could feel her body pulse in response.

"Zack," she whispered. "Please."

She couldn't believe those words had come out of her mouth. She couldn't believe she'd meant them. Emily had never been a sexual person; she could go for months without so much as a single sexual thought. But being with Zack like this, wanting him with such intensity, was driving her to do and say things she would have never imagined.

Then he was over her, smiling down at her, but there was an intensity in his face she'd never seen before. A serious look that told her there were no pretenses between them.

Lifting his hand, he brushed the hair from her forehead. "Open to me," he said. "Let me inside you."

She could feel her body thrumming, her heart hammering against her ribs. He entered her with devastating slowness. She felt her body melting around his as she was filled to the hilt. Sensation rose in a swift tide to sweep her away. Then he began to move, and pleasure exploded into ecstasy.

Her body moved in exquisite time with his. For the span of a heartbeat they were one. One body. One heart. One mind. One soul. And when the heat reached a fever pitch, Emily came apart in his arms, shattering into a thousand pieces that would never be put together in quite the same way ever again.

Chapter Fourteen

Zack watched her sleep and tried not to think about what he'd done. The fire in the hearth cast amber light onto her flawless complexion. Her mouth was full and partially open, and it took every bit of discipline he possessed not to take her in his arms and make love to her again.

Exhaustion tugged at him, but Zack knew he wouldn't sleep. His mind was too troubled. He'd slept with a woman while in the midst of a dangerous mission. Again.

Sometimes late at night he swore he could still hear the shot that had killed Alisa...

Restless, he rose and slipped into his pants. The cabin was chilly so he piled wood in the hearth. Then he walked to the window looking out over the snowy forest and tried to think of a way to salvage the mission. Instead he found himself cursing fate for sending this woman to him when there was no way in hell he could have a relationship with her.

"Zack?"

He started at the sound of her voice and turned to find Emily standing a few feet away. She was wearing her uniform shirt. Silhouetted against the yellow light from the fire, she looked slender and lovely and so tempting his heart ached just from looking at her.

"Go back to sleep," he said, surprised by his hostile tone.

She cocked her head. "What's wrong?"

"I need to think and I can't do it with you standing there half-naked."

She blinked as if she didn't understand. When she started toward him, his temper flared. Couldn't she see that this couldn't lead anywhere? Couldn't she see that the last woman he'd touched during a mission had died because of him?

Then her arms were around him and he felt the contact penetrate all the way to his bones. Need and desire coiled tightly inside him. He fought them, but his arms went around her anyway. When she fell against him, he set his chin against the top of her head and closed his eyes.

"I shouldn't have let this happen," he said.

"A lot of things shouldn't have happened in the last two days, but I don't think you were in control of any of them."

He drew away and eased her to arm's length. "I shouldn't have been with you like this, Emily. I'm in the midst of a mission, for God's sake." Releasing her, he turned back to the window and rapped his hand hard against the sill. "Damn it."

"Zack." She started toward him.

"Stay the bloody hell away from me," he said.

She stopped. "I don't understand where this is coming from."

He spun to her and immediately wished he hadn't, because seeing her only made him want her and that ticked him off even more. "I'm trying to keep you safe, Emily. If something happened to you…"

"Nothing's going to happen to me," she said.

Angry because she was tempting him and he damn well didn't want to be tempted, he crossed to her. He gently held her. "I've seen it happen. I've seen innocent people shot down. I've had friends killed because of me. I don't want that to happen to you."

"What are you talking about?"

"I'm talking about Alisa Hayes."

It was the first time he'd spoken her name aloud, and it struck him so hard he nearly staggered.

"I don't know who she is," she said.

"She's the woman who died because of me."

"Zack, calm down…"

He could feel his hands trembling. His heart pounded like a piston in his chest. Staring into Emily's pretty eyes, all he could think was that he would give his own life to keep her safe.

"Tell me what happened," she said.

Even after two years it hurt to speak about that night. It hurt because Zack knew her death was his fault. The old pain taunted him. Guilt churned in his gut. He could feel himself shaking. His hands. His legs.

"She was an operative with MIDNIGHT." His voice was so rough he barely recognized it. "We were to infiltrate a terrorist group that had set up camp in the west Texas desert. They were smuggling weapons through Mexico and selling them on the black market in the U.S. and Canada. MIDNIGHT got involved when Internet chatter indicated they were planning to sell material for a dirty bomb to a terrorist group with plans to hit a major Southwestern U.S. city."

"I never heard of any of that."

"Nobody ever hears of any of the things MID-NIGHT gets involved in."

"What happened?"

Zack laughed. "What didn't happen?" he said, his voice sounding caustic even to him. "Everything that could have gone wrong did." Remembering all too clearly, he tasted bile at the back of his throat. "This was a dangerous group, Emily. One wrong move and they would take you out into the desert, bind your hands and shoot you execution-style."

"You infiltrated the group?"

"It took us a year, but Alisa and I were finally in. We were accepted by the group. We were relatively comfortable." His mouth curved into a humorless smile. "As comfortable as you can be living with thirty murderers with sociopathic tendencies.

"We knew something big was about to go down, but the kingpin kept the details close to his chest, telling only a couple of his closest associates what it was."

"It sounds like you were doing exactly what you'd been sent in to do," she said.

"I did a hell of a lot more than I'd been sent in to do." Zack shook his head. "Alisa was a thrill seeker. Just about everyone at MIDNIGHT gets off on adrenaline in one form or another. But Alisa was…over the top. We were camped about fifty miles east of El Paso. Most of us used tents. The kingpin was so paranoid he slept in an underground bunker. Most of the weapons were stockpiled in underground bunkers, as well. So there we were, in the middle of the godforsaken desert, scared and bored and surrounded by killers. And Alisa…we were friends, you know? I knew her well. I liked her. Respected her as an agent. She was good at what she did, and we worked well together. Then one night she just showed up in my tent. I was sleeping. When she came in, I thought something was wrong. I went to her and the next thing I knew…" Remembering, he gritted his teeth. Being with Alisa Hayes had been like jumping off a cliff and landing hard. "We were together for the first time that night."

"Zack, you had been working under extremely stressful circumstances for a long time. I don't think it's terribly unusual for two people to turn to each other at a time like that."

"It didn't stop after that night, Emily. She came to my tent every night. I knew I should stop her. I was getting distracted. She was, too. I couldn't keep my mind on the mission because I kept thinking about her. I was beginning to…I was starting to care for her." Feeling the old pain twisting in his gut like a dull knife, he closed his eyes. "But I couldn't stop. We were burned out. Scared. Lonely. Being together was the only thing keeping us sane."

His gaze met hers. "By the time I realized I'd fallen in love with her, it was too late."

LOVE.

The word rang hollowly in the confines of the cabin, and Emily felt it like a physical punch. The slow, uncomfortable burn of jealously singed her. She knew it was small and petty of her to be jealous of a woman from Zack's past. Especially when the woman was nothing more than a ghost that haunted him. But she was.

"What happened to her?" she asked.

Turning away, he crossed to the hearth to stare into the flames. "MIDNIGHT had provided us with a radio transmitter so we could report in occasionally. We kept it inside an airtight trunk, buried in the ground a couple of miles from the encampment. We were supposed to check in every couple of days. Report any activities or plans. Let our contact know we were all right. Because it was risky, I usually did the contacting. I'd do it at night. Sneak past the patrols and steal away from the camp on foot. I could cover two miles in about nine minutes. I had a hand shovel buried beneath some rocks. It took me about a minute to get the case out of the ground. I would set up the antenna, spend about two minutes passing along whatever information I could. Then I would bury everything, hide the shovel and get back into the camp without ever being discovered. It was a relatively good system."

"It sounds incredibly dangerous," Emily said.

"It was." Zack scrubbed a hand over his face. "One night when she'd come into my tent, I told her we had to stop. I told her we were compromising the mission. We were distracted." His expression was tense. "We had a fight. She stormed out of my tent. I let her go, thinking we needed some time to cool off. I had no idea she was going to go to the radio."

"Why did she go to the radio?"

"She'd had enough. She was burned out and wanted to quit the mission."

"What happened?"

He sighed. "A shipment of weapons had come in just that afternoon. Neither Alisa nor I realized that night-vision goggles were part of the shipment or that the guards were wearing them that night."

"Oh, Zack."

"It was my job to know what kind of equipment was coming in, Emily. Guns. Explosives. High-tech devices. Whatever. It was my job to know." Setting his hand against the mantel, he leaned. "I woke to voices a couple of hours after she left my tent. One of the guards had seen her leaving the compound and followed her. They caught her using the radio."

"Oh, no." Emily's heart began to pound because she knew what he was going to say next.

"They dragged her back to the camp and woke the leader, a man by the name of Guy Hind. I stood just outside my tent while they questioned her. Alisa was belligerent and tough as nails. She didn't tell them squat." His voice broke off and he seemed to struggle with what he needed to say next. "And so they began hurting her."

Emily could see his hands clenched into fists. Sweat beaded on his forehead. He was blinking his eyes rapidly, as if trying to erase from his mind the images of his lover being tortured. "I kept hoping she'd gotten through to our contact at MIDNIGHT, that they would send someone in before things got out of hand. But not even MIDNIGHT could get a team there fast enough to save her. And I knew I had a decision to make. I could either save her life and blow the operation. Or I could let her die and salvage what was left of it."

He raised tortured eyes to hers. In their depths Emily saw deep and terrible pain.

"I ran back to my tent and grabbed my weapon. I was outnumbered twenty to one, but there was no way I could let them kill her." His voice was so low and hoarse that she had to lean close just to hear him.

"I had the son of a bitch in my sights when he pulled the trigger," he said.

For the first time Emily felt the sting of tears in her eyes. She could see the same pain etched into

Zack's every feature. It was a pain that was a part of him. An agony he'd accepted into his psyche and learned to live with.

"I felt that bullet go through her as if it had gone through me," he said. "They shot her execution-style. She was killed instantly."

"My God."

"I figured I was next, but I wasn't going to go down without a fight."

"How did you get out?"

"Avery Shaw, who is my boss now, was an operative back then. Alisa had indeed gotten through to her contact at MIDNIGHT. Within minutes a chopper dropped a team of five men. Shaw was in charge and got me out, but he took a bullet in the spine that ended his working in the field."

"Everyone else got out alive?" she asked.

"Everyone except Alisa."

"And you blame yourself."

"I'm the only one left to blame."

She couldn't imagine the horror of what he'd seen or the pain he must have felt. The crushing guilt. "That's why you've been so determined to protect me from the people at Lockdown."

His gaze burned into hers. "I'm determined to protect you for a lot of reasons."

She stared at him, conscious that her heart was doing acrobatics in her chest, that her pulse was thrumming.

Crossing the short distance between them, he set

one hand on her shoulder, touched her cheek with the other. "I care about you, Emily. I care too damn much and I honestly don't think I could handle it if you were hurt because of me."

"I'm not going to get hurt. What happened to Alisa was not your fault."

"Don't," he snapped.

"Zack, we've come this far—"

"And this is as far as you're going to go, Emily. It's over."

She blinked. "What are you saying?"

"I'm going to drive you to the next county and turn you over to the police. You'll probably be arrested, but at least you'll be safe."

Anger surged inside her. "Like hell you are."

"If you stay with me, you're going to get hurt, damn it. I'm not willing to risk that."

"The decision is not yours to make."

"I'm not taking you with me."

She wanted to know where he was going and what he had planned next but couldn't ask the question. Not until she'd convinced him she would be going with him. "You are not in charge of my life. You're sure as hell not in charge of what I do."

"I'm in charge of this mission."

"I am not going to walk away from this, Zack."

"I can't take you with me!" he shouted.

"I'm not Alisa!" she shouted back.

For several long seconds he stared at her as if she'd slapped him.

"Don't shut me out," she whispered. "I need to

do this. I need to help you. I need to help myself. Please don't take that away from me."

The next thing she knew, his arms were around her and he was crushing her body to his. His mouth sought hers. She tasted desperation and lust and a hundred other emotions she couldn't name.

And then she couldn't think of anything except kissing him.

ZACK COULD FEEL THE KISS pulling him in a direction he didn't want to go. But he was tired of fighting it. He was tired of fighting his attraction to her. He kissed her hard, keenly aware that she was kissing him back, that her body was flush against his, that he was hard, his body aching to get inside her.

Growling low in his throat, he shoved her to arm's length. She stared at him, her eyes huge, her lips wet and kiss-bruised. And the only thought his brain could manage was that he wanted to kiss her again. He wanted to do a hell of a lot more than that.

"This is bloody crazy," he said gruffly, not sure if he was referring to the situation or the powerful attraction between them.

Emily assumed he was referring to the latter. "What's crazy is the fact that you won't let me help you because you're hung up on something that happened in the past."

"Or maybe I'm one of those smart people who learn from their mistakes."

"You're not going to change my mind," she said

breathlessly. "I'm going to see this through with or without you."

"What the hell is that supposed to mean?" he asked, grinding out the words.

She put her hands on her hips. "That means if you cut me loose, I'll do this on my own."

Chapter Fifteen

"Where are we going?" Emily asked.

They had been in the Jeep for half an hour, heading south, as best she could tell. Because of the snow, they seemed to be moving at a snail's pace, and it was maddening.

Zack looked over at her, his expression tense. He'd been silent and brooding since leaving the cabin. Emily knew he wasn't happy with her. But there was no way she was going to let him take her to the local sheriff's office to be arrested and detained while he risked his life to finish this alone.

"I thought we'd drive by Clay Carpenter's house," he said after a moment. "If the house is dark, I'll slip inside and see if I can find something that will connect him to Signal Research and Development."

Denial rose swiftly inside Emily. She'd known Warden Carpenter for fifteen years. Her father had worked for him. He'd helped her land the corrections officer position with Lockdown, Inc. He was a good man, a fair man.

"Zack, I've known Warden Carpenter most of my life. I don't think he's involved."

"Two days ago you thought the same thing about Marcus Underwood."

"Maybe Underwood is running the show and Warden Carpenter doesn't know anything about it."

"If that's the case, he doesn't have anything to worry about, does he?"

She was about to continue her defense when Zack punched off the headlights. She glanced through the thick trees and lightly falling snow to see Clay Carpenter's house. The place was lit up like a football stadium. Four pricey SUVs were sitting in the driveway. Normally Emily wouldn't have questioned so much activity; Clay and his wife, Jessica, frequently entertained. Emily had been there herself. But it was three o'clock in the morning. At least two of the SUVs were from Lockdown, Inc.'s fleet....

"There's something going on," Zack said.

"Maybe he's entertaining a few colleagues."

"Yeah, and maybe that red SUV parked behind the Chevy isn't the one we saw at Signal Research and Development."

"What?" Emily squinted out the window. Astonishment shot through her when she realized the red SUV was the same one they'd seen back at Signal Research and Development. The one with the dented fender.

"That ties Carpenter to Signal," Zack said.

She didn't want to believe it. But then, Emily hadn't wanted to believe a lot of things Zack had proved to her in the last hours. Had she been wrong about the warden, too?

Feeling sick inside, she pressed her hand to her stomach. Warden Clay Carpenter. He'd been her father's best friend. She couldn't believe he would be involved. But from all appearances he was.

She wanted to rage at the betrayal. At the unfairness of the situation. The ruination of her career. An innocent man like Zack being pursued by every law-enforcement agency in the state.

Innocent.

For the first time it struck her that she now believed everything he'd told her. About his being an undercover agent. About MIDNIGHT. About Lockdown, Inc. and the Bitterroot prison. That he was innocent. All her lingering doubts were finally put to rest. The realization was heady. And it made her even more determined to end the killing and make things right. She knew in her heart there was only one way.

"We need to go back to the prison," she said.

Zack had already pulled back onto the road. He nearly drove off the shoulder when she made the suggestion. Catching the wheel just in time, he swerved back onto the snow-covered asphalt and shot her an incredulous glare. "Don't you think it would be a lot easier if we just found a gun somewhere, put it to our heads and pulled the trigger?"

"Is that Zack the MIDNIGHT operative talking?" she asked. "Or is that man who lost his lover two years ago?"

Cursing, he flipped on the headlights and turned the Jeep onto a narrow back road where the snow was deep, the trees thick. "It's the man who just happens to have enough sense to know when he hears a bad idea," he snapped, braking the Jeep and jamming it into Park.

"Getting into the prison is the only way we're going to break this thing wide open," she said.

"What makes you so sure of that?"

"Because I still have my keys. I know the security codes—"

"Most high-security facilities change codes and locks when there's a breach."

"That's a pathetic excuse not to try."

"Your idea is suicidal, Emily."

"The prison is the last place they'll expect us."

"That's because they've made the incorrect assumption that you're sane!"

"Zack, you know I'm right. The proof we need is in the prison."

"I'm not going to let you do it."

"If you want to complete your mission, if you want to stop the brutalities occurring in that prison, if you want to stop Warden Carpenter and Marcus Underwood and Dr. Lionel, you will."

"If I decide to go back in, I do it alone."

"I have the codes. I know where Marcus Underwood's office is. I know he keeps all of his vital information on the computer in his office. I know the layout of the buildings."

"So do I," he snapped.

"You don't know about the underground passages."

"What the hell are you talking about?"

"I'm talking about the underground passages leading to the Special Housing unit. The tunnels are still under construction. Nobody uses them yet. The contractors are still working on the project."

Zack had seen blueprints of the Bitterroot facility. How could his superiors at MIDNIGHT have overlooked something as critically important as underground tunnels?

"How do you know about the tunnels?" he asked.

She shrugged. "I've taken the main tunnel before. As a shortcut. I was running late and had to get to the Special Housing unit."

"Terrific," he muttered, but his mind was reeling with the implications. "What makes you think the tunnels will be at all helpful?"

"Because they make the perfect escape route if we get into trouble."

Zack felt her words like a noose around his neck being drawn inexorably tighter. He stared at her in the dim light coming off the dash, awed by her courage and beauty. Taken aback by his feelings for her. Terrified because she was right.

"It's the only way," she said.

For the first time in his professional career panic descended and he felt it all the way to his core. There were too many things that could go wrong. Too many people involved. Mainly a pretty brunette with eyes that could bring a man to his knees with nothing more than a look. Right now Zack was that man. On his knees and at her mercy, because he couldn't bear the thought of her being hurt.

"Don't do this," he said, grinding out the words. "Not after what happened to Alisa."

"You know I'm right," she said. "Please, I know my way around the prison. We can get in easily, get the proof we need and then get out before anyone realizes there's been a security breach."

Frustration made him want to break something. He didn't like having his back to the wall. He sure as hell didn't like having so much at stake. Cursing her and wanting her with an intensity that was maddening, he reached out and pulled her to him.

"Damn you." He could feel his need for her digging into him. The heady rush of blood pooling in his groin. And he couldn't believe he could want her at a time like this, when everything was tangled and wrong. But he did. More than his next breath.

Pulling back slightly, he gazed into her eyes. "If anything happens to you—"

She pressed her finger to his mouth, silencing him. "Nothing's going to happen," she whispered. "I promise."

It took every bit of discipline he possessed to pull away, but somehow he managed. Mechanically he started the engine and put the Jeep into gear. Five minutes later they were on the highway, heading toward the Bitterroot prison.

It was then that he remembered Alisa's last words to him had been chillingly similar to Emily's.

HALF AN HOUR LATER, ZACK stopped the Jeep in a deserted mountain town that consisted of a ramshackle motel, a defunct gold mine and a gas station touting an oil change for sixteen ninety-nine. Leaving Emily in the Jeep, he went directly to the pay phone at the service station.

He knew he was taking a risk by making the call. But there was no way he and Emily could walk into the prison without some backup. Zack did the only thing he could think of and circumvented his usual point of contact.

The operatives at MIDNIGHT were never to contact any fellow agent or superior at home. But Zack had never played by the rules; he knew a call to the agency would lead to another ambush. And so he broke every rule in the book and went directly to the top of the organizational chart. He called Avery Shaw at home. Breaking protocol would probably cost him his job, but he figured that was a hell of a lot better than getting himself—or God forbid, Emily—killed.

He'd known Avery Shaw for five years. He was a good agent, a good man. He'd been there the night Alisa died. He'd talked Zack down when Zack had been on a very precipitous edge and about to leap. He'd been the one to contact Alisa's family. He'd picked Zack up off the floor when Zack had been too drunk to do it himself. He'd treated him like an agent when Zack had felt as if he would never be able to work again.

"Shaw." A sleep-roughened voice rumbled on the other end of the line.

"This is Devlin."

A long, pregnant silence ensued. "What the hell are you doing calling me at home?"

"Trying to save my ass, no thanks to you."

"What is that supposed to mean?"

"That means you have a mole within your ranks, mate. A mole who just about got me bloody killed."

Another meaningful silence ensued. "Who is it?"

"I don't know. I called my regular contact to set up a meet. And I got ambushed. Thought you might want to know."

"Hell, yes, I want to know."

Zack heard rustling on the other end of the line and imagined the other man getting out of bed.

"I'm pulling you out," Shaw said.

"Like hell."

"Let me remind you of something, Devlin. I'm calling the shots. I say you're out and you're out. You got that?"

"I didn't spend four months in that hellhole to walk away empty-handed," Zack said.

"And I don't feel like having to bury another agent!"

Zack closed his eyes briefly at the mention of Alisa but said nothing.

"Pull out now," Shaw snapped, "or I swear I'll bring charges against you."

"We're going into the prison tonight."

"Damn it, Devlin, that's a suicide mission. Don't do it."

"I thought you should know in case we don't come out. We're going for the big dogs, Avery, and big dogs bite."

"You connected someone at the top?"

"Yeah, and we're going to bring them down."

"We? For God's sake, don't tell me you're talking about Emily Monroe."

Zack had anticipated Shaw figuring out he and Emily were working together, but it didn't make him feel any less a fool. "Don't do anything that will get us killed, Avery."

"I'll leave the getting killed part up to you!" Shaw shot back. "You know there are two other operatives in the prison. They can help if you get into a tight spot."

Zack figured he was already in as tight a spot as a man could be and not get squeezed to death. "As far as you know, one of them is the mole."

"No way."

"Do me a favor and don't bet my life on it, okay?"

"I'm going to personally bring charges against you when I get my hands on you."

"If I'm still alive, it's a deal." Knowing the other man had already begun tracing the call, Zack smiled and disconnected.

Chapter Sixteen

"Who was that?" Emily asked when he got back into the Jeep.

"An old friend."

"Odd time for you to call an old friend."

Zack said nothing and he didn't meet her gaze.

"If you're trying to be subtle about evading my question, you're not doing a very good job of it."

"Let's just say he's a friend who's good at picking up the pieces."

She thought about that for a moment and tried not to let it frighten her. "We're not going to need anyone to pick up the pieces because we're not going to get caught."

"That's the spirit."

"I mean it, Zack. We can be in and out in twenty minutes—"

"If some corrections officer walks in on us with a shotgun, it's over," he said angrily.

Emily stared at him, aware that her pulse was up, that she was frightened and uncertain and suddenly having second thoughts about what they were about to do.

"I made that call because if we don't get out of there tonight, I don't want Underwood or Carpenter or anyone else getting away with our murders."

A queasy shudder moved through her. "You don't think we're going to make it out."

"I think we're bloody insane," he said and rammed the Jeep into gear.

TWENTY MINUTES LATER, Emily slid out of the Jeep into knee-deep snow. They had parked on a narrow back road a couple of miles from the prison. "Why are we stopping here?"

"Unless you want to tango with the perimeter patrol guards, we cover the last two miles on foot," he said.

Emily had been scared plenty of times in her life. Having spent the last three years working as a corrections officer in a high-security prison, she'd learned to work through her fears. Staring down at the lights of the prison in the valley below, she'd never been scared like this before. She couldn't shake the feeling that something was going to go wrong. She couldn't discuss it with Zack because she knew there was nothing he'd like better than to turn around and leave if only to keep her out of the line of fire. That was the one thing she could not allow.

"We approach from the south," he was saying.

Emily looked over at him. Even in the darkness

she could see that his expression was grim. He was staring at her, his mouth pulled into a thin line, his jaws clenched tight.

"We use the trees for cover," she managed.

"I cut the fence in the northwest corner."

"That's right beneath the guard tower—"

"Where they can't see us," he cut in.

"But how are we going to get from the guard tower to the main building?"

He looked up at the sky. "I believe Mother Nature is going to give us a hand."

Emily blinked, not understanding. Then it dawned on her that it was snowing. He was planning to use the snowfall as cover.

"How do you know the snow is going to continue?" she asked.

"I don't." He stared at her for an instant. "I'd feel a hell of a lot better about this if you stayed here with the Jeep."

She didn't miss the worry carved into his every feature. Emily hated being responsible for it, but there was no way she could sit this out and let him go in alone. "I'm going in with you," she said.

His jaw flexed, and he looked quickly over his shoulder. "In that case, we'd better get going."

Zack set a swift pace, and even though Emily was in top physical condition, she had a difficult time keeping up with him. He took her down a steep ravine, through a forest of sapling ponderosa pines, a frozen creek and at last to the edge of the open meadow where the prison had been built.

In a matter of minutes he had the coil of concertina wire cut. "We're going to sprint along the line of trees that runs along the driveway," he said. "From there we take cover beneath the tower. No more talking. Follow my hand signals from here on out. Got it?"

Emily nodded, but she could feel her entire body vibrating with a combination of adrenaline and fear and the daunting knowledge that if either of them made a mistake now, it would cost them their lives.

"Let's go."

The snow was falling heavily as they sprinted alongside the row of trees. Emily ran as fast as she could, staying slightly behind Zack, conscious that he kept himself squarely between her and the guard tower fifty yards away.

They reached the tower without incident. The base of the tower was cinder block. A blue steel door led to the interior and, she assumed, a stairwell that led to the observation deck. Taking her hand, Zack led her to the north side of the building—away from the door—and pressed her to the cinder block. "So far, so good," he whispered, looking over his shoulder.

Emily was about to push off when he turned to her. His eyes latched onto hers and held. Within their depths she saw all the same emotions that had been raging through her own mind in the last minutes. Fear of discovery. Worry for someone she cared for deeply.

When his gaze flicked to her mouth, she knew he

was going to add one more emotion to the mix. Then he was crushing his mouth to hers. A hot spike of desire drove right through the middle of her. Even through the fear and adrenaline she could feel her body responding. Every nerve ending tingled with the heady sensation of being kissed by Zack Devlin. She could feel her muscles quivering, her mouth seeking his, her body beginning to ache.

When he pulled away, his eyes were black and intense, his pupils dilated with passion. Brushing his hand along her face, he gave her a half smile. "Let's go."

They crossed the courtyard at a reckless speed. Snow stung her face and eyes. Emily was mindful of the spotlights flashing on the building to her left. They stopped in the alcove just outside the side entrance to the cafeteria and skidded to a halt.

"Which door?" Zack whispered, but his eyes were scanning the alcove, darting to the courtyard beyond.

"There's a door the nutritionist and her staff use. Near the cafeteria. It should be deserted this time of night."

"Where?"

She pointed. "Right. About twenty yards down."

"Let's move."

He followed her directions and soon they were standing outside a steel door painted an institutional blue. Zack turned toward the courtyard while Emily swiped her security card, then went to work on the code. Seconds later the locks clanged.

"They didn't change the codes," she said. "We're in."

"God help us."

They entered the kitchen, a massive room chock-full of gleaming stainless-steel counters, matching sinks and a massive freezer and refrigeration unit. The lighting was dim, but Emily could see well enough to make her way down the aisle.

"Nice kitchen," Zack commented.

"Only the best for Lockdown, Inc." She took him past a set of stainless-steel ovens built into the wall, then to the door that would take them to the corridor leading to the main building. "Where do you—"

Her words were cut off abruptly when the door swung open. Emily gasped when she found herself face-to-face with a corrections officer.

"Monroe?" He looked at her as if she had come back from the dead. "What are you doing here?"

She couldn't remember his name. He was new. Fresh out of the police academy, but he hadn't made the cut, if she remembered correctly. Alan. Or Andrew. "Oh, hi," she said, wondering where Zack had disappeared to.

"I thought you were—"

He didn't have the chance to finish the question. Zack plowed into him from the side and took him to the ground. The officer made a feeble attempt to regain control but in a flash Zack had the nylon restraint off the man's belt and his hands cuffed behind his back.

"Hand me that towel," Zack said.

Emily's heart was still in her throat as she snatched the towel off a rack and passed it to him.

"Sorry about this, mate." Zack stuffed the towel in the man's mouth and knotted it at the back of his head. Rising, he then dragged the officer to a nearby pantry, dropped him inside and closed the door.

"Cooks are going to have quite a surprise when they open the pantry door and find Barney Fife instead of their pancake mix," he said.

Emily pressed a hand to her stomach. "My God, Zack, what if he'd been more experienced and gotten to his weap—"

"He didn't," Zack snapped.

They faced each other. Emily knew he wouldn't admit it, but she could see that the incident had shaken him. She could feel the tension coming off him. And for the first time she admitted to herself that coming here was a mistake. They were outmanned and outgunned. She figured the odds didn't get much worse.

"I should have listened to you," she said.

Reaching out, he set his hands on her shoulders and squeezed. "We're going to be okay."

Her gaze clashed with his. "If something happens to you, it's my fault."

"This is nobody's fault except the monsters running this place." Giving her shoulders a final squeeze, he looked toward the door. "Can you get us into Underwood's office?"

"I think so."

"What about Carpenter's?"

"Two doors down from Underwood's."

Zack must have seen something in her eyes because he tilted his head and looked at her closely. "What?"

"We have to pass by the infirmary to get there." A new thread of worry curled in her gut. "It's manned 24-7."

"We've got to try." He grimaced. "If something goes wrong, I want you in those tunnels. No looking back. You got that?"

There was no way she would ever leave him behind. She started to nod, to appease him, but he suddenly grasped her arms and gave her a gentle shake. "Promise me, Emily," he growled. "Damn it. I mean it."

She stared into his eyes and wondered if he had any idea how much she had come to care for him. "I promise," she said.

He gave her a smile, but it held little humor. "Well, then, let's do a little breaking and entering and see what we can find."

Taking her hand, he pulled her through the door and into the corridor. They jogged at a fast clip, their boots muffling their steps on the tile. At the end of the hall, Emily started toward the elevator, but Zack pulled her into the stairwell, and they went down the stairs to the lower level.

The basement was cold and dimly lit. A sign on the wall read: Infirmary. An arrow beneath the word pointed to the right. They were three-quarters down the hall when a scream stopped them dead in their tracks. It was a sound of terror and agony rolled into a single horrific sound. A man reduced to an animal.

"Oh, no." Emily glanced at Zack. "My God, what are they doing to him?"

His face was filled with disgust. "The bastards are testing their poison on some convict because he's bloody convenient and free of charge."

Another scream shattered the silence. A high-pitched wail. "My God, Zack, we have to help him."

She started down the hall. An instant later Zack's fingers bit into her shoulder. Knowing he was going to try to stop her, Emily spun on him, ready to fight.

The look in his eyes took the fight right out of her. "We can't let them torture a human being to death," she said.

"We're not going to be any help to him if we're dead," Zack said firmly.

Another agonizing scream punctuated his words. Unable to keep herself from it, Emily put her hands over her ears. "I can't stand it."

"You rush in there unarmed and with some half-baked idea of saving that poor bastard and you'll end up strapped to a gurney yourself."

Zack squeezed her arms. "Listen to me. We need to stick to our plan. It's the only way to help these men."

Blinking back tears, she concentrated on pulling herself together.

"We need to get into Underwood's or Carpenter's office," Zack said. "We don't have much time."

Giving herself a hard mental shake, Emily stepped

away from him and pointed down the long hall. "Dr. Lionel's office is one level up."

"Let's start there."

IT TOOK ZACK LESS THAN thirty seconds to pick the lock. Once inside Dr. Lionel's office, he went directly to the desk and began to ransack it. He could hear Emily paging through the files in a nearby cabinet. In the last drawer he searched, he found what he was looking for.

"Look at this," he said, pulling a bound notebook from its nest.

Emily left the file cabinet and crossed to him. "What is it?"

"Diary of a madman," he said dryly.

She leaned close to read the handwritten notes of how each individual convict had reacted to the RZ-902.

Patient A-4922B, thirty-six-year-old male, 180 lbs., 5'11". Patient was placed in the chamber at approximately 3:03. By 3:04, the RZ-902 had begun to work. Intense discomfort was observed, followed by skin lesions, bleeding from the nose and mouth and eyes. Four minutes into the treatment the patient suffered respiratory arrest and was rendered unconscious. Death occurred one minute later....

Zack had seen a lot of terrible things in the years he had been an agent. Not much bothered him anymore. But the cold-blooded premeditation of what was happening here made him feel sick inside, made him furious.

"My God, Zack, this is incredibly…vile."

She was standing so close he could smell the sweet scent of her hair. He could feel the goodness and warmth coming off her. And suddenly he needed to be reassured that those things still existed. Putting his arms around her, he pulled her close and closed his eyes tightly.

For several heartbeats neither of them spoke. Then Zack looked into the depths of her eyes. If anything happened to this woman, he would never be able to live with himself.

Struggling to rein in his emotions, to concentrate only on the mission, he tore the pages from the notebook, folded them in half and stuffed them into the waistband of his pants. "Let's see what we can find in Underwood's office."

Leaving Dr. Lionel's office exactly as they had found it, Zack and Emily sprinted down the hall toward Underwood's office. The area was well lit. He picked the lock as quickly as possible, knowing that if someone rounded the corner, they would be in plain sight. Thirty seconds later he was inside Underwood's inner sanctum.

The office was furnished with dark, glossy furniture. The wall to Zack's right was filled with books and volumes and legal tomes. Straight ahead, a computer sat atop an intricately carved desk.

"Underwood keeps everything on his computer." Emily went directly to the desk and switched it on.

"He'll have a log-in ID and password," Zack said, following her.

"Everyone at Lockdown, Inc. has a similar log-in ID." She settled into the chair behind the desk.

Zack watched her fingers play across the small keyboard, but he was uncharacteristically nervous. He couldn't stop looking at the door. Couldn't stop imagining all the things that could happen if someone walked in and caught them. Feeling sweat break out on his back, he glanced at the clock on the wall. Not yet 5:00 a.m. They still had some time before people started showing up for work. But they'd been inside for fifteen minutes. Another ten minutes and they were going to have to make a run for it whether they had what they needed or not.

"Damn it."

He looked down to see Access Denied flash on the screen.

"I found the log-in ID, but not the password," she said.

"What did you try?"

"He's got two kids. I tried both names."

"Try his wife," Zack suggested.

Emily's hands flew over the keys. Access Denied flashed.

"Any pets?" he asked.

"No."

"Maybe it's case sensitive," he said. "Try capitalizing the first letter of each name. Then add a number, starting with one and working your way up. You have ten minutes, Emily."

Keys clicked as she tried again. "No go," she said.

Zack could feel desperation pressing into him.

He'd known before coming in that finding the proof they needed to connect both Underwood and Carpenter to the testing of illegal weapons was a long shot. The notes would help, but it wasn't enough to convict. There were no names, nothing written on Lockdown, Inc.'s letterhead, nothing to connect Lockdown to Signal Research and Development. He needed definitive evidence. He wanted it so badly he could taste it.

But the longer they stayed, the better their chances of getting caught. If it were only him, he would risk it. But because he couldn't bear the thought of Emily being hurt, he found himself willing to walk away empty-handed if that's what it took to keep her safe.

"There's got to be another way," he said.

"I need more time," she said.

"Finding that password is a long shot, Emily."

She glanced away from the keyboard, her determined gaze colliding with his. "I know him, Zack. I know his administrative assistant. He keeps everything on this computer. If I can get in, we'll have him cold."

"It's not worth your life, damn it."

She looked back at the keyboard, her fingers playing over the keys at a blinding speed. Zack was about to reach for her to physically haul her from the room when she gasped. The screen blinked and a blue menu appeared.

"I'm in," she said.

Relief penetrated the veil of fear that had been

about to choke him. "You've got two minutes." He glanced uneasily toward the door. "I'll search the desk and file cabinet."

Anxiety churned in his gut as he crossed to the file cabinet and went to work on the lock. He could hear the computer keys clicking as she worked. The occasional curse. Then the file cabinet lock snapped and the drawer rolled open. Starting with the first file, he began to read. Most were medical files on inmates. The inmate was identified with a number, not by name. The information looked legit. Nothing about RZ-902.

"Oh, my God."

The tone of her voice snapped Zack's head up. Emily was sitting behind the desk, her face ghostly in the semidarkness. "I think I just found what we were looking for," she whispered.

Zack came up behind her and looked at the screen.

"This is the project-tracking software Lockdown, Inc. uses. My God, Zack, the entries...they're graphic and horrendous and..."

"And it details dates and names," he added.

She hit another key and the next day's log materialized. *Problem encountered with subjects resistant to RZ-902. Profuse hemorrhaging. Blindness. Skin lesions. Survival rate 68 percent with injection of antibody serum within the first minute of exposure. Dr. Lionel will begin another trial next week. Lockdown, Inc. will supply volunteers at $5,000 each.*

"Shall I print this?" Emily asked.

Zack reached over and switched on the printer. "Print it and then I'll e-mail a copy of the entire file to a couple of private accounts I have set up." Leaning close, he used the mouse to open the e-mail software and then typed in several e-mail addresses. "Delete the e-mail in the Sent folder. If we're lucky, they won't figure out we were here."

Emily clicked on the Sent folder and deleted the e-mails he'd sent. She opened another file. Zack saw names and amounts and his heart began to race.

"We've got them," she whispered.

The rush of relief hit him with a force that was almost physical. Zack looked down at her and grinned. "Kind of renews a man's belief in miracles, doesn't it?"

Pulling her from the chair and to her feet, he cupped the back of her head and pressed his mouth to hers. Desire tugged at him as he kissed her. He could feel himself getting lost. Getting too close. Too deep. Too damn fast. He wanted to think it was his love affair with danger and adrenaline that had him breathless. But deep inside he knew it was the woman he held in his arms.

The printer spat a dozen pages and beeped. It took every bit of discipline he possessed to pull away. "Remind me not to kiss you when I need to think."

"Same goes," she said, looking more than a little shaken.

Zack crossed to the printer, snatched up the sheets, folded them and tucked them next to the other pages in the waistband of his pants. "Let's blow this joint," he said.

"We can take the tunnels," she said. "They'll be faster and we'll be less likely to run into anyone."

He'd just reached for her hand when the door swung open and he found himself staring at four men, all of them holding high-powered rifles aimed at his heart.

Chapter Seventeen

Emily saw four men with guns, each muzzle trained on Zack. She could feel high-octane adrenaline pumping through her entire body.

"Move and I'll put a bullet in his heart," one of the men said. "Get your hands up. *Now!*"

She stared at the men, unable to believe this was happening. They'd been so close to getting away. One of the men strode toward her.

"I said get your hands up!" he shouted.

"Emily," Zack said. "Do it."

Snapping out of her shock-induced stupor, she raised her hands.

"Put your hands on the desk and spread your legs," one of the men said to Zack.

She watched as Zack complied, wondering how he could be so calm about this. The men roughly patted down Zack, then seized the folded papers from his waistband.

"You, too," one of them said to Emily.

Emily didn't want them touching her but didn't think she had a choice.

"Do what they say," Zack warned.

Before she could obey, a sandy-haired man with cold blue eyes shoved her against the desk. "Put your hands on the desk." He kicked her legs apart, then quickly and impersonally searched her.

"She's clean."

"We've got Devlin and Monroe," one of the men barked into his radio.

Zack shot a hard look at Emily. "You set me up, you bitch," he said loudly.

It took her a moment to realize the crude words were an act so the corrections officers would think he'd kidnapped her.

Doing her best to play along, she straightened and turned to face the officer who'd patted her down. "I didn't think you'd ever get here."

"Put your hands back on the desktop," the officer snapped. "Now!"

Heart pounding, Emily obeyed. Dear God, they didn't believe her.

"I forced her to bring me here," Zack said.

"All of us have seen the security-camera videos, Devlin." The sandy-haired man grinned in Emily's direction. "Don't tell me you haven't had a piece of her." He sneered at Emily. "Must have been pretty damn good to give up the rest of your life for a convict."

Emily glanced over at Zack to find his eyes already on her, urging her to stay calm. She wanted desperately to believe they were going to get out of this, but she didn't see how.

Movement at the door drew her attention. Everything inside her froze when Marcus Underwood strode into the room. His eyes sought Emily and he shook his head as if he were supremely disappointed.

"Why couldn't you just do your job and stay the hell away from this?" he asked.

She stared at Underwood, her heart thumping like a drum against her ribs. She thought of the screams she'd heard in the infirmary and a fierce hatred for him surged up. "You're a murderer," she spat.

"*Emily,* that's enough."

She heard the warning in Zack's voice, but her emotions were out of control. There was no way she could heed him. Not when the man she'd respected her entire professional life was responsible for untold misery and murder. "We know about the RZ-902," she said. "We know you're using the inmates as guinea pigs. We know the people at Lockdown, Inc. are about to sell it on the black market."

A chill passed through her when Underwood smiled. "How astute of you."

"You won't get away with it." She tried to make her voice strong, but it was trembling all the same. "We've already sent some of your files via e-mail."

Underwood snapped his fingers at one of the men. "Contact our IT people and have the server taken down. Now."

One of the men nodded, then fled the room.

Underwood's eyes flicked to Emily. "What else do you think you know?"

"I know you're not going to get away with this. I know there are people who are on to your sick research project."

Zack moved toward her, set his hand on her shoulder. "Emily, don't—"

Suddenly the officer nearest Zack swung his rifle like a baseball bat. The butt slammed against Zack's solar plexus. Air whooshed from his lungs. Zack doubled over, choking back nausea as his knees hit the floor.

"Zack!" Forgetting about the men holding guns on them, she rushed to him and dropped to her knees at his side.

"Don't say anything else," he said through gritted teeth.

His entire body shook with the effort of trying to get oxygen into his lungs. She looked up at Underwood. "What do you want?"

"I want you to disappear," he said. "Both of you. Permanently."

He was going to kill both of them. Oh, dear Lord, how were they going to get out of this?

Zack raised his head, his face filled with fury. "The entire world knows about your operation, Underwood. It's all about to come crashing down around you."

The opening of the door drew Emily's attention. Relief burst through her when Warden Carpenter entered the room. He would stop Underwood. The police would rush in and take the prison administrator into custody. She was about to go to him when his gaze met hers. Relief turned to horror when she realized he was part of this.

"Warden Carpenter," she said dully.

His gaze went from her to Zack, then back to her. "Sleeping with the enemy, Emily?"

"Please tell me you're not part of this."

"Ah, loyal to the end." The warden crossed to her and set his hand against her cheek. "Such a shame you have to die because of it."

"Stay away from her, you twisted son of a bitch." Next to her Zack struggled to his feet, his eyes black with fury. "Your little empire is about to collapse."

"My empire, as you so aptly put it, Mr. Devlin, is alive and thriving. I can have all evidence of any wrongdoing removed in a matter of an hour or so. Remember we do have a crematorium on-site." He looked at Emily and one side of his mouth curved. "The RZ-902 is a roaring success, by the way. In fact, I've already got buyers lined up."

"You sold out your country. You murdered dozens of people," she said disgustedly.

"Come now, Emily," Carpenter cut in. "Who am I killing? Murderers? Rapists?"

"They're human beings," she choked. "Men who've been sentenced to prison, not a life of torture."

"Most of these men have committed atrocities," Carpenter said with sudden passion. "Men who will never be a productive part of society."

"You have no right," she said.

"That's where you're wrong. I do have the right.

You see, the criminal justice system gave me the right."

Zack gazed at him with utter loathing. "You're selling weapons of mass destruction to terrorist organizations. You not only sold out your country, mate. You sold your soul."

"My soul is my business." The warden shrugged. "The rest is for Homeland Security to worry about. I'm merely a businessman."

"You're scum." Emily tried to launch herself at him, but Zack moved quickly to grab her wrist and haul her back.

"Easy," he whispered.

Carpenter contemplated her a moment, his expression amused and oddly affectionate. "You are your father's daughter, aren't you, my dear Emily?"

"I'm nothing like my father," she said evenly.

"You are more than you realize. Adam Monroe was an idealistic fool." Carpenter rubbed his chin thoughtfully. "It's a shame you never knew the truth about him."

"I know all I need to know."

"Did you know he stumbled upon the preliminary plans for RZ-902 when we were working out of the women's correction center? What has it been, fifteen years now? Did you know he found out we had done some preliminary experimentation on a few of the female inmates? Did you know he threatened to go to the police?"

Emily felt the words like a blow right between the eyes. Dazed, she stared at a man who'd been her father's best friend. His professional ally and advocate. A man she'd trusted.

"I don't know what you're talking about," she whispered. "My father committed suicide. H-he was with a female inmate."

"I'm afraid we had to eliminate poor Adam," Carpenter said. "He was a good man. Too good. I hated destroying that squeaky-clean reputation of his. But I couldn't let him take what he knew to the police, now, could I?"

She could feel her heart pounding wildly in her chest. Disbelief and fury rising in a violent tide. "Easy, Emily. Let it go," Zack said quickly, touching her arm.

She shook off his hand. "I don't believe you."

"Yes, you do. I see it in your eyes." Carpenter shook his head. "We gave him a choice, you know. Join forces with Lockdown, Inc. or face the consequences." He shrugged. "He made the wrong decision."

Tears stung her eyes, but she blinked them back. "You murdered him."

"We made it look like suicide, of course. I'm afraid we also had to permanently silence the female inmate." A smile whispered across his face. "She was the first of many."

Emily couldn't believe her ears. For fifteen years she'd believed her father had disgraced the uniform he'd worn by having a relationship with a female inmate. She'd believed he'd committed suicide instead of facing up to his mistakes. In reality, he'd been trying to stop the same madman she and Zack were.

"You're a monster," she said.

"I'm a businessman," he said, unfazed. "I have a product to develop and sell. When problems get in the way, I remove them." He looked from her to Zack, then back to her. "You and Devlin have become a problem, Emily." His eyes were as gray and cold as ice. "You see, the new generation of RZ-902 has not yet been tested on a female subject. We suspect there will be slight differences in the way the female nervous system responds."

A chill went all the way to her bones when she realized what he was saying. She could feel the tremors moving through her body.

Raising his hand, Carpenter snapped his fingers. "Take her to the testing chamber." He turned his gaze on Zack. "Take him directly to the crematorium and burn him alive."

ZACK HAD ALWAYS BEEN GOOD at getting out of dire predicaments. He'd saved his own life and the lives of others by the skin of his teeth on more than one occasion. But for the life of him he didn't know how he was going to get them out of this one. For the first time he seriously considered that both he and Emily would be killed, and no one would ever be the wiser.

Three men were holding high-powered rifles on him. Marcus Underwood was standing near the door. Clay Carpenter was standing a few feet away from Emily. Zack couldn't take his eyes off her. He couldn't think of a single thing he could say or do that would stop what was about to happen.

From where he stood, he could see her trembling. He could see the rapid rise and fall of her breasts. He could hear the hiss of her breaths coming short and fast. When her gaze met his, he saw the terror in its depths. He wanted to touch her, to comfort her, to let her know everything was going to be all right. That he was going to get them out of this. If only he knew how....

"Let her go," he heard himself say. "Take me. I'll go willingly. I'll do whatever you want. Just let her go."

Carpenter and Underwood exchanged knowing looks, then Carpenter spoke. "She is lovely, isn't she, Devlin?"

Zack met the other man's gaze levelly. "Let her go."

Carpenter grimaced, looking appropriately distressed. "I'm quite fond of her myself. But she knows too much."

Zack wanted to rip the other man's heart out. He could feel the rage rushing through his veins. He could feel his fists clenching with the urge to strangle Carpenter right then and there.

He used his last resort. "The agency I work for will hunt you down. They will not stop until your twisted scheme is as dead and buried as you."

Every muscle in his body tensed when the door opened. Zack glanced over. Shock jumped through him at the sight of Avery Shaw. Surprise gave way to confusion when he saw Shaw was alone. That he wasn't armed. Then the truth hit him. Shaw had not come here as part of the MIDNIGHT team to break up an illegal weapons-testing facility.

"I see you've got everything under control." Shaw's gaze went to Zack.

It wasn't often that Zack was totally surprised. But he was now. The realization that his friend Avery Shaw was the mole struck him like a sucker punch. "You're the mole," he said.

"Of course."

"Why, Avery?"

"Let's just say I owe you." Shaw's gaze went from Zack to Emily, then back to Zack. When Zack said nothing, Shaw shook his head. "Come on, Devlin, you're quicker than that, aren't you?"

Zack's mind whirled with possibilities, but he couldn't think of a single reason why Avery Shaw would double-cross him and get an innocent civilian killed in the process. It just didn't make sense.

"I loved her, you know," Shaw said.

The situation crystallized. The truth pummeled him like a thousand fists. "Alisa Hayes."

A dark emotion flashed in Shaw's eyes. "She and I were together. Then you stepped in and…you took her from me."

Zack scrubbed a hand over his face. The pain of a friend's betrayal cut him. "She came to me, Avery."

"Lying bastard. You seduced her. You…slept with her. Then you got her killed, damn you."

The old guilt churned even as Zack denied it. "I didn't know."

"They had to dig a bullet out of my spine because of you," Shaw continued. "The doctors didn't know if I'd ever walk again. Do you have any idea how difficult it was to leave the field to sit behind a desk? Do you have any idea how painful a spinal injury can be to a man?" He looked at Emily, a malicious smile spreading across his face. "I must say, this is one instance where the revenge is going to be sweet. I'm going to hurt her, Devlin. I'm going to enjoy watching you suffer."

"Don't do this, Avery," Zack warned. "Enough people have died. Stop this now."

Shaw glanced at the sandy-haired man with the rifle. "Cuff him. Cuff his feet, too. Watch him closely. He has a black belt."

Marcus Underwood nodded. "I'll have Dr. Lionel sedate them so they'll be easier to handle."

Shaw shook his head. "I don't want them sedated," he said coldly. "I want Devlin stone-cold sober when she starts screaming. I want him to hear her. Then I want him burned alive." Hatred blazed in his eyes as he gazed at Zack. "I've waited two long years for this. By God, I want it to be worth the wait."

Never in a hundred years would he have suspected Avery Shaw. The man had saved his life. He'd been a friend and confidant. Zack knew the spinal-cord injury had been hard on Shaw. But he never would have imagined the other man taking it to this level.

Zack looked at Emily and a different kind of guilt began to roil inside him. She stared back at him, her eyes wide with terror, her face the color of paste. He couldn't bear the thought of her dying a long and painful death because of him. If he had to sacrifice his own life to save hers, he would do it.

He saw one of the men pull a set of stainless-steel cuffs from his belt. "Put your hands behind your back, Devlin."

"Run to the tunnels," he whispered to Emily out of earshot of the other men.

Tears shimmered in her eyes. "I'm not leaving you."

"I have a plan," he lied. "Now go. I'll find you."

"Give me your hands." The man with the cuffs grasped his arm and turned him roughly.

Zack spun, brought his right foot up and knocked the man out cold with a single kick. Lunging, he punched one of the armed officers with a palm-heel strike to the nose. The man's head snapped back, blood gushing. The man's rifle flew from his arms. Zack went for the rifle. Out of the corner of his eye he saw an armed man swinging his gun muzzle toward him. And Emily streaking toward the door.

Zack's fingers curled around the stock of the rifle. "Run!" he shouted to Emily and brought the gun up.

An explosion rocked his brain. For an instant Zack thought he'd gotten off a shot. Then the bullet seared into his side. Pain like he'd never felt before slammed through his body. An animalistic sound squeezed from his throat. But the pain was secondary to the terror, because in his peripheral vision he saw Underwood lunge at Emily.

Clutching his side, Zack watched her fight off Underwood. A rise of elation went through him when she reached the door, swung it open. *Run!* Then a guard caught her. Zack watched in dismay as her arms were jerked behind her back, her wrists cuffed.

Dear God, no, he thought.

Then the world faded to black.

THEY WERE GOING TO KILL HER. Emily knew that as surely as she felt the cold grip of the handcuffs around her wrists. But fear for her own life meant little to her in light of what had happened to Zack. She couldn't believe he'd been shot. That she couldn't go to him. That they were forcing her to leave him behind. Oh, dear God, she couldn't walk away!

She struggled with the men dragging her into the hall. She screamed and cursed at them, but her efforts were in vain. "Let go of me!" she cried.

"Stop fighting!" one of the men shouted.

Jerking away from the sandy-haired man, she turned toward Underwood. "They shot him. Marcus, please, you can't let him die. I'll do anything. Just…dear God, he was bleeding."

Another layer of horror and helplessness settled over her when Underwood only smiled. "Dear Emily, you've become quite fond of Mr. Devlin, haven't you?"

Closing her eyes against the pain of knowing

Zack was badly injured and at the mercy of a man who hated him, she nodded. "I love him. Marcus, please, I'll go willingly. Just…don't let him die."

For the first time Underwood looked uncomfortable. "It's out of my hands, Emily."

"No," she said, her heart breaking. *"No!"*

Underwood jerked his head at the sandy-haired man. "Just get her to the testing chamber."

ZACK LAY ON HIS SIDE watching his own blood pool around him. Considering he'd been shot, he didn't feel all that bad. The pain had faded to a dull, burning ache. He was dizzy and slightly nauseous, but by no means in agony.

Closing his eyes, he concentrated on the sounds around him. There was at least one person in the room. Zack didn't know who it was, but he was a lot more concerned with whether or not they were armed. He wondered if he was able to get up.

Only one way to find out….

Groaning involuntarily, he rolled onto his back. He doubled over, seized with pain so intense he thought he was going to pass out.

"Not a very good feeling to be helpless and shot, is it, Devlin?"

Shaw. Cold-blooded bastard. Zack opened one eye, found himself staring up at him. "No thanks to you," he muttered, surprised by the feebleness of his own voice.

"We got her, you know." Shaw squatted next to him, his elbows on his knees, and tilted his head to make eye contact. "She says she loves you, Devlin. What do you make of that?"

"Good taste in men," he said.

"A smart mouth to the end. Damn, I always respected you." Shaw rose. "But it's not going to help you. Or her."

"What about Michaels and Vanderpol?" Zack asked, referring to the undercover agents MID-NIGHT had sent to the prison with him. "Are you going to kill them, too?"

"They're in holding cells in the receiving area." Shaw grimaced. "You see, we're going to cover this up with a prison riot, Zack. Burn the bodies and the evidence. Truck the RZ-902 into Canada. And let the prisoners take care of the rest."

"Pretty clever for a psychopath." Zack watched him walk to the desk and pick up the set of hand-cuffs the security personnel had left behind.

"I think I'll just put these on you until they come back for you," Shaw said.

"I'm not going to do squat," Zack said, purposefully making his voice sound even weaker. "I'm bleeding out. Why don't you just sit back and enjoy the show?"

Shaw smiled, but his expression remained bitter. "Maybe I will. After I cuff you." He walked over to Zack and squatted. "Turn over on your stomach and give me your hands."

"Okay, just…" Zack groaned, let his voice trail. "Give me a minute, will you?"

"Not a chance." Roughly, enjoying Zack's pain a little too much, Shaw forced him onto his stomach.

Zack used the momentum to roll. Before Shaw could respond, Zack brought up both legs and plowed his feet into the other man's chest. Shaw reeled backward. Zack leaped to his feet. Dizziness stole through him, but he quickly shook it off. Before Shaw could rise, Zack landed another kick to the other man's chin. Shaw's head snapped back. Another punch to his jaw sent him sprawling to the floor. Snatching up the handcuffs, Zack closed one end around Shaw's wrist, the other end to the file cabinet drawer pull.

"That ought to keep you for a while," Zack muttered as he started toward the door.

Hatred seethed in the other man's eyes. "You'll never get out of here alive."

"Maybe not," he said, "but at least I'll have my soul."

Chapter Eighteen

Emily tried every self-defense tactic she'd learned in the course of her training, but she was no match for the two large men dragging her toward the gurney.

"Get her onto the gurney!" Marcus Underwood ordered from his position near the door. "Strap her in."

Strong arms wrapped around her forearms from behind. Another set of arms closed around her calves. Emily twisted and tried to lash out with her feet, but the two men were well trained and amazingly strong. The next thing she knew, she was being lifted and placed on the gurney.

"Help me!" She screamed as one of the men began securing the straps. Thick nylon restraints were stretched taut over her legs. Two over her torso. Another around her neck. Two more for each arm. She was totally immobilized.

She didn't want to think about what would happen next.

Marcus Underwood looked down at her and shook his head. "You should have minded your own business, Emily."

"Don't do this, Marcus," she pleaded. "It's not too late to stop this."

The other man's expression was strained. But there was no comfort in knowing he wasn't enjoying this. "Wheel her into the testing chamber," he said. "Let's get this over with."

Emily threw her head back and screamed. She cried out Zack's name as one of the men pushed the gurney into a stark, windowless room tiled from ceiling to floor. The sandy-haired man kicked down the brake on the gurney so it would stand in place. Then he left the room.

Emily stared up at the ceiling. She could feel the panic pulsing inside her. A scream building in her chest. Tears stung her eyes when she thought of Zack. He'd been shot. Trying to save her. Oh, please, God, let him be all right….

"That will be all," she heard Underwood say. Then he was standing over her. Terror spread through her when she saw the tiny vial in his hand. "Do you want me to explain to you what's going to happen?" he asked.

"I want you to let me go."

He pursed his lips. "I'm going to leave this vial in the room with you. The waxy outer core will begin to melt when the room temperature reaches eighty degrees. It will take the wax approximately four minutes to melt. Once that happens, two billion particles of RZ-902 will be released into the air. Within seconds you will ingest enough into your lungs to shut down your central nervous system. Your mucous membranes will bleed. There will be some skin irritation. Headache. Abdominal pain."

"Don't do this." Emily panted with fear.

"I don't have a choice." He dropped his gaze, then crossed the room to a small tiled table and set down the vial. "I'm sorry, Emily," he said. "I'm very, very sorry."

"No!" she screamed. "You can't do this!"

The door slammed. The lock turned.

"Oh, God. Oh, God!" She struggled against the straps binding her, her body bucking, but her efforts were futile. She thought about Zack and her heart broke.

"Please be all right," she choked. "Help me."

Then it was just her and the vial and the terrible wait for a slow and agonizing death....

ZACK SPRINTED TOWARD THE door at the far end. He'd always perceived physical pain as an issue of mind over matter. But then, he'd never been shot in the side before. Pain racked his body every time his feet hit the ground. He was bleeding profusely and leaving bloody footprints. A trail very easy to follow....

But he wasn't going to let any of that stop him. He had to keep Underwood and his thugs from killing Emily.

Hang on, his mind chanted as he covered the ground at a swift pace.

He loved her. He'd loved her since the moment he laid eyes on her. Because of the circumstances he just hadn't realized it, or maybe he just hadn't been brave enough to acknowledge it. And now she could be dying....

The thought of losing her filled him with pain ten times worse than any gunshot wound. Every time he closed his eyes, he saw her face. Her smile. The way she'd looked at him after he'd kissed her. The way her eyes had glazed when he'd been inside her. Emily Monroe was decent and good and kind. The world needed her. *He* needed her. There was no way in hell he was going to let her die.

At the end of the corridor Zack paused. He was sweating profusely, his face burning as if with fever. He set his hand against his aching side, felt the sticky ooze of blood. He looked down and his palm was slick and red.

"Damn it," he muttered, leaning against the jamb and willing his head to clear.

He needed help. If he passed out or was captured before reaching Emily... *No,* he thought. He wouldn't let himself go there. He had to reach her. If it was the last thing he did, he would get her out of here.

Voices reached him through the haze of pain. Clutching his side, Zack backtracked a few steps and slinked into the alcove of a doorway and peered down the hall. A male corrections officer was walking toward him, speaking into his radio as he approached. He was looking down at the bloody footprints on the floor.

"Subject has definitely been this way. Blood looks fresh. Advise. Over."

"Roger that. Subject is armed and dangerous. Approach with extreme caution. Lethal force has been authorized."

"Roger. Out." The officer shoved the radio into its sheath as he passed the alcove.

Zack waited until the man had taken two steps past him before he crept from the alcove and tapped him on the shoulder. The officer went for his pistol as he spun, but Zack was prepared. A palm-heel strike to the nose sent the man sprawling backward. In a flash Zack was on him. A single punch to the solar plexus and the man was incapacitated. Using the man's own cuffs, Zack quickly secured his hands, gagged him and relieved him of the pistol and radio.

"Don't mind if I borrow these, do you?" he asked and left the officer groaning on the floor.

But the physical exertion took a heavy toll. Dizziness and nausea washed over him as he entered the prisoner receiving area and closed the steel door behind him. The sergeant's desk was vacant. He passed by it and paused outside the prisoner holding area. Peering around the corner, he spotted the sergeant with the two operatives Zack had been sent in with.

Kendra Michaels was wearing a skirt and heels, her right wrist cuffed to the bar embedded in the wall above the bench. Jake Vanderpol was already in a cell. From where Zack stood he could see that the other man's face was bleeding and he knew Jake had put up a fight.

Feeling the press of time, Zack silently entered the room. Kendra made eye contact with him, then moved quickly to gain the attention of the sergeant. "I have to go to the bathroom," she said.

"Too bad," the man snapped.

"That's no way to treat a lady." Zack jammed the pistol against the sergeant's spine. "Unlock those cuffs or I'll put a bullet in your back."

The sergeant went rigid, his hands shooting up.

Zack reached for the man's pistol and handed it to Kendra. "I think you can put this to better use than he can."

Smiling, she trained the gun on the sergeant's heart. "Get these cuffs off me," she said. "Now."

The sergeant's hands shook as he unlocked her cuffs. "You won't get away with this."

"Watch." When the cuffs were released, she motioned toward the cell where Jake Vanderpol was standing. "Open it," she said to the sergeant.

"What the hell took you so long?" Jake said as the sergeant unlocked the door. Then he noticed the blood on Zack's side and grimaced. "Jeez, Devlin, you're leaking like a sieve."

"How bad?" Kendra asked, coming up beside him.

Zack didn't care about his own gunshot wound. "They've taken Emily Monroe to the testing chamber," he said. "I've got to get to her before they release the RZ-902."

"You're in no condition to be saving anyone, Devlin." Kendra shoved the sergeant into the cell and slammed the door.

"She's right, Devlin," Jake said.

"I don't have a choice," Zack said and started toward the door.

"What the hell are we waiting for?" Jake said to Kendra, and the three of them went through the door as a single combined force.

THE DRIPPING OF THE MELTING wax onto the tile tormented Emily. For the first time in her life she was totally consumed with terror. She felt every heartbeat like the ticking of a death knell.

From where she lay bound she could see the two-way mirror. She wondered if Marcus Underwood, Clay Carpenter and the man from MIDNIGHT who'd betrayed Zack stood on the other side, gaining some sort of perverse satisfaction from her impending death.

Zack.

A sob broke from her lips when she thought of him, of all the things they would never do together, of all the things that would never be. Even though she would die here today, she would at least go to her death knowing she'd loved with her whole heart, body and soul.

That would have to be enough.

The wax had stopped dripping.

Emily choked back another sob, closed her eyes and waited for the pain to begin.

ZACK DIDN'T BOTHER WITH a warning when he burst into the testing chamber receiving area. He took out the security officer with a single shot to the head. The man dropped without even looking up. Kendra darted to the fallen man and quickly confiscated his weapon. Jake Vanderpol headed toward the administrative offices. Pistol drawn, Zack sprinted down the narrow corridor toward the observation room. Darkly tinted glass was set into a tiled wall. A red light flickered In Use, and he knew Emily was inside.

I'm too late.

The thought besieged him as he barreled toward the glass. He couldn't bear the thought of her dying. She was the only thing that mattered. Not his own life. Not justice. All he wanted was for her to be alive, because he couldn't imagine the world without her.

"Devlin, don't!"

Zack heard Jake's shout, but he didn't hesitate. Using his coat to protect his face, he hurled himself through the glass. The window shattered on impact. Shards flew like razor-sharp pieces of ice. Then he was inside the small tiled room. Emily was strapped to a gurney. Tears streamed from her eyes. A cry tore from her throat when she raised her head and saw him.

"Zack! *No!* Run! The RZ-902—"

"Quiet." Slashing the straps with his knife, he pulled her from the gurney. The urge to take her into his arms was powerful, but Zack knew the gas may have already been released into the air.

"Devlin, get out of there!" Jake bellowed.

But Zack was already pushing Emily through the shattered observation window, then following her through. On the other side Jake Vanderpol put a pistol to Marcus Underwood's cheek. "You have two seconds to tell me how to neutralize that gas or I'm going to throw you in that room and let it take you to hell."

Underwood's eyes bulged, his throat worked convulsively. "W-we modified a fire extinguisher, filled it with a neutralizing agent."

Kendra Michaels crossed to the red extinguisher, yanked it from its hook on the wall, then hopped through the broken window to spray the melted vial of RZ-902.

Zack couldn't get Emily far enough away from that hellish room. He let her help him, but only because he liked the way it felt when she put her arms around him. Besides, he was a little dizzy. A tad nauseous. He made it as far as the prisoner receiving area before he collapsed.

"Zack! My God, you're bleeding."

"Just a flesh wound," he said.

Emily went to her knees beside him. "It's bad."

Jake was already on the phone. "Care Flite chopper is en route. ETA ten minutes. Hang tight, buddy."

"Hope they bring food. I'm starved."

Choking out a sound that was part laugh, part sob, Emily took his face in her hands and kissed him full on the mouth. "You saved my life."

"Just doing my job."

"You did a lot more than your job."

"You're right. I wouldn't take a bullet or jump through a glass window for just anyone." He smiled, but it was becoming a struggle to keep his eyes open. "But I'd do it all over again for you."

She closed her eyes briefly, and tears began to roll down her cheeks. "I didn't want to die without telling you I love you."

"Thanks for clueing me in," he said. "That's one hell of an incentive for a guy to pull through when he's shot."

"There's a hundred more where that came from, Zack Devlin."

"I'm feeling better already." But he could feel consciousness slipping away. He didn't want to leave her. He wasn't sure if he'd be able to find his way back. And she was so damn good to look at.

"I'm here." She grasped his hand and squeezed hard. "Zack. *Zack!* Don't you dare die on me."

"Wouldn't dream of it," he murmured and drifted into space.

Epilogue

One week later

Emily stood in the cold Idaho wind, hugging her leather coat against her, and stared down at her father's headstone. Kneeling, she set her hand against the date of his death. "I owe you an apology, Pop," she said.

The trip to the cemetery was long past due, but this afternoon was the only time she'd had in the last week to come here. She'd spent most of the last week at the Boise Memorial Hospital with Zack while he recovered from a serious bullet wound. The rest of her time she'd spent with different branches of law enforcement and even the brass at MIDNIGHT, answering questions and making statements as they tried to recreate the events that had led up to the showdown at the Bitterroot prison the night she and Zack had nearly died.

Avery Shaw, Marcus Underwood and Clay Carpenter were in jail, each of them awaiting trial on various charges that would keep them behind bars for the rest of their lives. Thanks to Zack.

She looked at the granite headstone and smiled. "And you, Dad. I'm sorry I doubted you all these years. You were a hero, and now I'm going to make sure your contribution to ending the horrors of RZ-902 are officially recognized."

"I might be able to help with that."

Emily rose and spun at the sound of the familiar voice. Then she was staring at Zack Devlin and the rest of the world melted away. He'd lost weight in the week he'd been hospitalized. His face was pale. But he was smiling, and at the moment it was exactly what she'd needed.

"I didn't know you were being released," she said.

He arched a brow. "I hurried the doc along a bit. I bloody hate hospitals."

"Me, too."

He motioned toward the headstone. "I told the people at MIDNIGHT about your father. What he did. They'll see to it that his name and reputation are cleared."

"Thank you."

An uncomfortable silence fell between them. Emily could feel her heart pounding. Even though she couldn't meet his gaze, she felt his upon her, digging into her, searching for something she wasn't certain she wanted him to see. She was torn between running to her car and driving away and throwing herself into his arms. She'd never been in love before, but she knew this moment was profound. Whatever happened here today, she knew it would affect her the rest of her life.

ZACK KNEW BETTER THAN TO push a woman like Emily when she didn't want to be pushed. But he'd been patient for a week now and she still hadn't given him any indication as to what was going through her mind. The not knowing was killing him.

"When I woke up and you were gone, I didn't know if you'd come back," he said.

She met his gaze, and Zack was taken aback by her beauty, by the courage he saw in the depths of her eyes. Most of all, he was taken aback by the sheer power of his own feelings for her.

"I didn't know if you wanted me to come back," she said.

He stared at her, wondering how she could not know that he was crazy in love with her. "The nurses told me you didn't leave my side for three days."

"You saved my life, Zack. I wanted to make sure you were going to be okay."

"Is that all?"

She blinked, then her gaze skittered away. "I don't know what you want me to say," she said. "We haven't talked about…the future."

"The future is what we make it."

"Your base of operations is in Washington, D.C. My life is here in Idaho."

"I suppose for two people in love that could present a problem."

The words, so simply spoken but so chock-full of meaning, went through her like a blade. Emily gaped at him, then choked out a laugh. "It does," she managed. "But I don't know what comes next. That scares me."

"Why does it scare you?"

"Because I'm in love with you."

His jaw flexed, like steel under tremendous pressure. When she'd professed her love after he'd been shot, he'd wondered if it had just been an extreme reaction to everything they'd been through together. But now as he gazed into her loving eyes, he knew that they hadn't just been words to see him through his medical ordeal. They had come straight from her heart.

He crossed to her in two resolute strides. Her eyes widened an instant before his fingers wrapped around her arms. Then he was pulling her to him. His hands tangled in her hair. He breathed in her scent, let the sweetness of it fill his lungs. He caught a glimpse of her startled expression, but he couldn't wait any longer and crushed his mouth to hers.

The kiss was long and slow and languid. The way he wanted all their kisses to be. Now and forever. "I love you, Emily Monroe," he whispered.

Putting his hand gently beneath her chin, he forced her gaze to his. "I've never loved anyone the way I love you. I'm not going to give that up without a fight, so if you have any ideas about ditching me, we had better have it out right here and now."

"But your job with the agency—"

"Is such that I can live in any city I please as long as there's a decent airport." He grinned. "I think the airports in Boise will suffice just fine."

She blinked rapidly but not before Zack saw the tears building. "I hope those are tears of happiness," he said.

She laughed. "They are."

"Good, because I'm not finished." Using his thumbs, he brushed the tears from her cheeks. "While we're on the subject of us, I thought I'd go ahead and ask you to marry me."

"You really know how to keep a girl on her toes, don't you?"

"Wouldn't want you to get bored with me."

"Not a chance, Zack Devlin."

"Is that a yes?" he asked.

"That's a resounding yes."

Feeling his emotions rising powerfully to the surface, Zack laid his forehead against hers and closed his eyes. "You just made me the happiest man in the world," he said.

"I'm just getting warmed up," she whispered and raised her mouth to his.